Sexy Sara

A Fifty Plus

2020 Romance


Author- B. J. Etheridge

# Chapter 1

Sara sat at the table outside the coffee shop. She was hot and tired and just wanted to get home. Her physical therapy appointment had been at one, it was now half past four and she still had no ride home. The thought frustrated her and brought tears to her eyes. She couldn't even take care of herself. Damn she was so pathetic.

Her year had not started out great. On January first she had been on her way to the movies alone when she got into a car accident. She had broken her ankle and her wrist, had to have surgery on both then spent the first two months of the year in a rehab facility. That had been a nightmare. They didn't have enough staff and hadn't done a great job of taking care of her. She couldn't put weight on her ankle or wrist for six weeks meaning she couldn't do much for herself. She couldn't come home because her son Robby had to work and couldn't be home to take care of her. Her daughters also had families to take care of, so she had stayed in the rehab facility. She was supposed to be getting physical and occupational therapy on her hand and wrist, but they had not done much with it.

Finally she was able to come home the first of March, just in time for the governor of Arizona to put everyone in quarantine because of COVID 19. It was a pandemic all over the world and everyone went into quarantine. She was supposed to have a nurse come in to help but the rehab facility had referred her to a company that didn't take her insurance.  It had taken another five weeks to get her directed to the right place.

That had meant no physical therapy and she could only shower if her son Robby was home in case she fell. She did manage so that she didn't have to embarrass Robby by making him bathe his mother. By the time they got it all worked out she no longer needed the nursing services.  She still couldn't use her hand very well so she was referred to outpatient therapy.  The new therapy office had gotten the referral from her doctor but they were not seeing patients because of the COVID pandemic. Her surgeons nurse had found this place for her and so she had started therapy on her hand.

Since she had wrecked her car in January, she no longer had her own transportation.  Luckily her insurance would pay to get her to doctor visits.  She had no other way to get to doctor visits so she had to put up with the insurance cab.  The problem was that they were having some major computer issues and they would either get her to her appointments too late or forget to pick her up afterward.   She had been left stranded so many times but when she complained it didn't seem to do much.

She sighed.  It looked like they had forgotten her again today.  She had been sitting here for two and a half hours.  It was a crime that they could leave disabled people stranded all over the city with no way to get home.  As she sat there feeling sorry for herself, she let the tears fall.  It was just so unfair. She had never felt so alone in her whole life.  She sat for a few minutes with tears streaming down her face then she took out a tissue, wiped her tears and regained control.

At five, she called Robby.  He was working from home but still had to be on the computer for his normal shift.  His shift ended at five so he could come get her after that.  Robby said he would definitely come get her it was only about five minutes away so she didn't have to wait long.  She decided not to cancel the cab, she wanted to see if they ever figured out the issue.  She was going to file another complaint with them on Monday and she needed to show that they never came to get her or even called to see if she had gotten home.

She was really tired of complaining.  It seemed like she was complaining after every appointment. She just didn't know how else to get the issues resolved.  Calling however, really didn't change anything.  They did the same thing the next time they had to pick her up.

Just then Robby showed up and she hobbled out to his car with her cane.  At least it was Friday and she could rest over the weekend.  She was going home to put ice on her wrist and ankle and rest.  They were to the point of throbbing after sitting out here for three hours in the sun waiting for a ride.

# Chapter 2

Charlie had not slept well last night.  His shoulder was still giving him a little pain and he had been up most of the night.  He slept in a little this morning thinking his physical therapy appointment was at ten, only to find out when he got there that it was at eight.  Luckily, they had still let him go through the exercises and get his therapy for the day, although the girls had teased him a lot about being late.

As he was going through the routine exercises, a lady came in for therapy.  He hadn't noticed her at first because his back was to the door.  As he worked his way around the room, he saw her sitting next to one of the tables doing hand exercises.  He could tell by the way she moved that they hurt and she didn't have great use of her hand.  When he finished the exercises with the weights, he decided to make friendly conversation.

"What happened to your hand?"

"I broke it in a car accident on January first.  They had to do surgery."

"Ouch, I broke my hand once.  That hurts."

That was stupid Charlie.  Make her feel like hers doesn't matter.

"I broke my ankle at the same time," she said. "They operated on that too and I spent the first two months of the year in a rehab facility."

"I'm so sorry.  A bad way to start the year. Hope you get to feeling better."

Just then the therapist interrupted.

"Are you ready for your massage?"

Charlie reluctantly moved over to the table.  He hadn't even had a chance to ask her name.

Charlie was getting physical therapy for a shoulder injury.  He had torn his rotator cuff and had to have surgery on it.  All in all his shoulder was doing pretty good and he was certain he would be out golfing again soon.  It was golf he missed the most.

While he lay on the table, the therapist massaged the sore muscles, and he thought about the beautiful lady sitting a few tables behind him.  She was older. Probably about his age, maybe a little younger. She was beautiful with dark brown hair and blue eyes. She wasn't wearing a ring, but that didn't always mean anything.  He wasn't sure how to proceed with finding out if she was single.  He didn't imagine that the physical therapist would tell him, that would be against HIPPA rules.  Hopefully, he would see her again and would get another chance.  The physical therapist finished the massage and put ice on it for him.

When Charlie was finished, he verified his next appointment, promising not to show up late again and he left.  Too bad he had to leave that little brunette behind without getting her name.

After physical therapy, Charlie stopped for a sandwich and then went home to work.  He was a portfolio manager and had quite a lot of work to do. He was lucky in the fact that he was able to work from home and set up his own schedule.  That had helped him go back to work earlier than if he had to go into an office every day. It had also helped with the COVID quarantine.  He had been able to stay home, rest and recover from his surgery while working.

Charlie started out answering emails and fixing issues but he couldn't forget about that cute little brunette.  He now wished he had at least asked what her name was.  All he knew was that some way he needed to figure out how to see if she was married and ask her out.

# Chapter 3

It was Monday.  Sara had physical therapy at ten this morning.  The cab company had picked her up on time so she was even a few minutes early to her appointment.  This had put her in a fairly decent mood.  She was sitting at the table working on the hand and finger exercises she had been given by the physical therapist.  It was quite monotonous and somewhat painful but needed to be done if she was going to be able to use her hand again. Touch the thumb to each finger, 1.2.3.4. 5.- 2,2,3,4,5. There were a few more people in the room today.  With the COVID virus, the physical therapy office had cut back their hours and spread patients out so they could try to keep everyone from getting sick.   That meant fewer people in the office at a time and everything was cleaned after each use. You also had to spread out so that you stayed away from each other.  Masks were required everywhere, social distancing of six feet was a must.  The gyms were closed.  Many restaurants were only open for takeout. A lot of people were working from home.

Sara had been away from people since January so not much chance she had it, but she also didn't want it, so she did wear a mask.  It was also a requirement by the physical therapy office.

As she sat doing her exercises, another patient, a man, probably close to her age, watched her do the exercises and then asked her what had happened.  He listened patiently then told her about his broken hand.  Probably just trying to let her know he understood her pain.  He was a nice looking gentleman.  He had white hair, cut close, he was probably a little bald.  His beard was also white, trimmed in the shape of a goatee. His eyes were deep blue.  She smiled back at him as they talked but of course it was hard for him to see her smile with the mask on.

He was there doing exercises on his shoulder.  He was talking the entire time, pointing out to the therapist how much better his shoulder was doing.  The therapist was giving him a hard time because he had been late for his appointment.  He said he had fallen asleep.  He finished his exercises, had a massage, and left after verifying the time of his next appointment.

Sara finished her exercises; the therapist massaged her arm and fingers, then put ice on it for 15 min.  After her visit was over, she headed to the coffee shop for a soda and a cookie while she waited for the cab to pick her up.  She had set pick up for 15 min after her appointment was over but they never made it on time, so she probably had plenty of time to eat.

Sara ordered two chocolate chip cookies and a soda.  She struggled a little with getting the soda since her hand was still immobile and she was trying to maneuver the cane with her left hand.  After a little struggle, she got everything out to the table outside the door.  She pulled out her phone and her kindle so she could read and watch for the text when her cab would arrive.

An hour and a half later, she had finished her cookies, drank the soda, and finished her book.  She sat back frustrated because it looked again like no one was coming to pick her up.  She called the insurance company to figure out what was going on.  Their automatic system didn't even show a trip for her.  She spoke to an operator and they requested the cab for her.  The driver called her within 15 minutes and she made sure they knew where she was located at in the shopping center.  She really hated these days.  They were physically draining on her.  It was past lunch time and she was hungry and tired besides the throbbing ankle and her wrist was sore from therapy.  She could have gone back in and ordered a sandwich but she really didn't have a lot of money to spend on eating out. The driver showed up.  She was not in the best of moods but tried to remember it wasn't the drivers fault.

When she finally made it home, she sat and rested for a few minutes then got up and made tuna for lunch.  She didn't feel like doing much with her hand.  She needed to take it easy this afternoon.

She finished lunch.  Now she felt better so decided to contact the insurance about her complaint.  They made all kinds of excuses.  Sara really didn't care. They were doing a crappy job of getting her to appointments. She told them she was going to have to call the insurance commission about them getting paid and not giving her service.

The rest of the afternoon, Sara worked on her website.  She had decided to write romance novels. She was able to type in a fashion using her thumb and middle finger on her right hand and the mouse in her left hand which had taken some doing since she was right handed.  She often hit the wrong keys and made a lot of mistakes but besides being very slow but she was able to manage.  The website and Facebook stuff was easier because it was mostly mouse work so she didn't use her right hand much.  She had started the writing because she needed a way to bring in money that didn't mean spending hours and hours sitting at a job and typing.  Her last job had made her type solid for eight hours a day and she just couldn't do that anymore.  She thought if she could get some books written and her name out there, she might actually be able to make residual money.  It would be slow, but hopefully it would work out.  It also helped her mood to write and do creative things for the book and her website.

After working for a few hours, she got up and put the chicken in the oven for dinner.  She and Robby had worked out a system.  She helped cook healthy meals and he helped her with the cutting and chopping that she had such a hard time doing after her hand injury.  It worked out well and wasn't too hard for her to accomplish.

# Chapter 4

On Wednesday, Sara had physical therapy early again.  She had finished her session and was sitting on the bench outside the coffee shop waiting for her cab as usual.  She saw the man from Monday, come in for his therapy appointment.  He noticed her sitting on the bench and waived as he walked towards the door.  She waived back.

An hour later, he came out after his session and she was still sitting on the bench.  He noticed her and walked toward her.

"Are you still here?"

"Yeah, I'm waiting for my cab."

"For over an hour?"

"Yes, it's set up by the insurance and they aren't doing a great job unfortunately."

"When will they be here?"

"I have no idea. Sometimes they don't even show up," she said, trying to hold back the tears.

She hated that she was so emotional about this but she felt so helpless.  He had noticed her sniffle a little but didn't say anything about it.

"Do you live far from here?" he looked up in the distance.

"No, about five minutes away."

He looked at her again, "I'd be glad to give you a ride if you need it.  I hate for you to sit out here in this heat if they aren't coming."

Sara agreed to the ride.  He seemed like a nice man and she was tired and hot and no telling when or if the cab would ever show up.  She also needed to get home an prop her ankle up before it started hurting again.

He introduced himself as Charlie Chambers.  Sara told him she was Sara Miller.  He held out his right hand to shake hers, but it was her right hand that was hurt, so she held out her left,

"Sorry, my other hand is the one hurt."

He chuckled and took her left hand.  He walked with her back to his SUV, taking her water bottle from her so she could handle the cane with her good hand and not have to carry the water in her right hand.  He opened the car door and helped her in then put her cane in the back seat.  After he got in on his side, he asked for her address and typed it into his GPS and they were off.

"So, are you married, or single?" he asked.

Sara explained that she was widowed, living with her son.

"That's a good boy to take care of his mother."

"Yeah, I raised him to be responsible and to take care of his family, I just thought it would be a wife and kids, not me."

"Well it works both ways.  You are lucky to have him help you."

"So what about you?" she asked, changing the subject.

"I'm an old bachelor.  Never been married, kind of set in my ways."  He didn't expound any further.

Just as they reached the corner of the next street, he turned and asked her if she was hungry and if she wanted to go to lunch.

A little surprised, she stuttered then said, "Yes, I guess I could go for some lunch."

"How about subway?  There's one right down here on the corner."

"That is fine with me."

He pulled into the parking lot and helped her out of the car again.  He sat her at the table outside and got her order before going inside to get their sandwiches.

In a few minutes, Charlie came back with the sandwiches and made a second trip in for the drinks. He sat down at the table saying that he was pretty sure he didn't have COVID.  He had been laid up with his arm for a couple of months.  Sara said she felt the same.  They took off their masks so they could eat.

Charlie looked down to see the glove she had on her wrist.

"Do you want me to get your sandwich out for you?"

 She looked up at him, "Yes, thank you." She said appreciatively. She then gripped the sandwich mostly with her left hand and then balanced a little with the thumb and middle finger on her right hand.

"What's the glove for?"

"It's an arthritis glove.  It helps keep the swelling down so it doesn't hurt so much. It also helps protect it when I'm out trying to get in and out of cars."

"Does it really help?"

"Yes, quite a bit."

"So explain how it happened again."

She explained about the car accident and that she wasn't sure exactly how she broke it but thought she might have put it against the dashboard as the cars hit.

She also told him it was the most pain she had ever felt in her life when she came out of surgery. The doctor was talking about going in to take out the brace but she wasn't sure about having the pain again.

"I'm so sorry," he said.

"Are you able to work?"

"No, lost my job because I can't type anymore. That is why I'm living with my son."

After lunch, they put their masks back on and Charlie took her home. Sara's son Robby lived in a nice condo.  Luckily, it was on the ground floor so she didn't have to worry about the stairs. Charlie pulled up in front of the condo and before getting out to help her he asked,

"When is your next PT visit?"

"It is at one on Friday."

"How about I pick you up at eleven forty five and we stop for lunch on the way?"

Sara gave him an embarrassed look. "You don't have to take me; I can take the cab."

"Oh, nonsense. They still haven't called you yet for today. I did notice that you didn't call them to cancel. You can't count on them and it isn't that far out of my way. I'll be here at eleven forty five."

"All right, if you insist." She smiled.

Even though he couldn't see the smile, he saw the sparkle in her eyes.

"I do," and he got out of the car and came around to help her out and up to the door."

She thanked him for the ride. He held gently to her arm and looked deep into her eyes. "No problem."

She could tell by the look in his eyes that he really didn't mind giving her a ride.  Sara could feel her face get red as she looked back at him.

# Chapter 5

After hearing Sara's story Charlie felt for her.  He couldn't imagine not being able to take care of yourself like that and then having to rely on the insurance to get you around when they seemed to do such a terrible job.  He noticed that she hadn't called to cancel the ride and no one had called to say they were coming.

He liked her.  Now that she was closer, he could see a little gray in her hair.  It was obvious she was coloring it because the gray was a thin line.  He couldn't judge, after all he was white and almost bald.  She still was beautiful and her eyes had a sparkle to them even with all her troubles.  They talked about his job.  He told her he was a portfolio manager.  He told her that he liked to golf and was hoping he could get back to that soon.  He was a little embarrassed to tell her how he hurt his shoulder when she asked. He had tripped and fell when taking the garbage out.  He had torn a rotator cuff and had to have surgery.  It was feeling better and he hoped he would be done with therapy soon.

He enjoyed talking to her and watched intently while she ate.  She had a sexy mouth.  He watched as she bit into her sandwich, getting mayonnaise on the side of her mouth then her licking it off with her tongue.  All he could think about was licking it off himself.  She had been looking at her sandwich but noticed him watching her eat.  Busted.  She smiled shyly and kept eating.

After taking her home, Charlie made sure Sara got into the house ok, then he headed back to the car.  As he drove off, he was glad he had given her a ride home.  He was thrilled to hear she was single.  He had enjoyed her company at lunch.  It had been a while since he had lunch with anyone fun.  Usually it was business lunches where you talked business and it wasn't as interesting.  She was a cute little brunette with green eyes and sexy as hell.  Sexy Sara, he laughed to himself.  He was glad that an opportunity had presented itself and he could drive her to and from physical therapy.  He would continue to do that as long as she needed just to have the opportunity to get to know her better.  His appointment on Friday was at two so he needed to see if he could talk them into changing it.  Then maybe he could change all the others to match up with her visits. If he couldn't, he was willing to make the extra trip.  He thought she was kind of cute.

On Friday, Charlie picked Sara up right at eleven forty five sharp.  He helped her out to the car and put her cane in the back.  He noticed how hard it was for her to get into the car.  She leaned a lot on her left hand and couldn't really hang onto the car with her right to steady herself.  He wanted to help but didn't know where to grab.  Finally he took hold of her elbow asking if that hurt her.  It didn't so he was able to steady her while she climbed in. He then climbed in, on his side, asking where she wanted to go for lunch.

"How about Jack in the Box. I've been dying for a sour dough jack burger."

Charlie laughed.  "Whatever the lady wants."

"How about the drive through?" he asked.  We will eat in the car and not have to be around a lot of people."

Sara agreed.

There was a park right across the street, so he drove over there and parked under a tree.  He left the car running with the air conditioning on since it was late May in Arizona and already getting hot.

They ate lunch while he asked about her kids and he told her about his niece and nephew.  He didn't have kids of his own, but he loved his sisters kids like they were his own.  He said, she was always mad about him spoiling them, but he didn't have anyone else to spend his money on.

He asked about her job.  She explained that she had worked in a call center where she was required to do a lot of typing, so since she could no longer type, they had let her go.

"So, what now?"

He knew right away that it was the wrong question.  She looked like she would cry.  But he had asked it, so he let it ride.

"Not sure yet.  I'm thinking about writing novels. Thinking that I can just type for a couple hours a day and take time off when I need to.  It will be a slow process but eventually I can write enough books and get a following and the money will just come in."

"What genre?"

She blushed before she faltered and quietly said, "Romance".

"Oh," he acted surprised.

"Why romance?"

"Because they are easy to write and people love to read them."

"Are you good in the romance department?" he asked teasingly.

"Oh, I have some ideas," She smiled and blushed at the same time.

After they finished eating, it was time to go to physical therapy.  He drove to the physical therapy office and then helped her out of the car.  It was easier to help her now that he knew he could take hold of her elbow.  She did lean on his hand but it seemed to help her a lot.  He had parked up close so she wouldn't have far to walk and they walked in together.

They both started their exercises and he asked the physical therapist if he would be able to change his visits to match Sara's.  The therapist looked at Sara to see if that was going to be ok.

Sara said, "Yes, that's ok.  He wants to give me a ride so it would be easier if they were at the same time."

They were able to change appointment times for both of them so they coincided enough that it wouldn't put Charlie out too much to give Sara a ride.

When they got to Sara's house that afternoon, Charlie helped her out of the car and walked her to the door to make sure she got in safely.  When they got to the door he asked,

"Do you want to go to the movies tomorrow night?  There is one of those pop up movie theaters at the ball park where you sit in your car.  I just thought it might be fun and something you could do that wouldn't hurt your ankle or your wrist."

Sara smiled, her eyes shining above the mask "I think that would be fun,"

"The movie is Aladdin if that's ok.  It starts at seven so we should probably leave 5:30 or so.  I'll go get popcorn from Harkins and we can stop at the convenience store for drinks and candy."

"Sounds fine.  I'll see you at 5:30 then."

Sara went in the house and Charlie stuck his hands in his pockets on his way back to the car.  He was as excited as a teenager on his first date.  He jumped in the car and headed up to Harkins theater to get popcorn.  He had seen them in the parking lot, selling

it to people as they drove through in their cars.
Amazing the things that were happening because of
COVID.

# Chapter 6

Sara spent a couple of hours Saturday morning writing.  She was serious about writing romance novels.  She also had not been completely truthful with Charlie.  She had checked into it a lot.  She had been listening to pod casts and reading training things she found online.  She knew she could write, but it was a whole different thing to get the books into peoples' hands who would read them.  That was what she was working on; getting a following and finding people that would buy her books.  She had set up a website, and page on Facebook as well as a group on Facebook.  She had almost a hundred people following her and she was having fun setting up posts with recipes, romantic sayings, and other fun things.  She even had a blog that talked about all things romance.

After lunch she decided to take a shower.  With her bad ankle and wrist, she was a little slow and her hair needed time to dry on its own since she wasn't able to blow dry and curl it.  She also decided to try and put on some make-up.  Charlie had seen her without make-up and didn't seem to mind, but she thought this tonight was more like a date than the rides to physical therapy so she wanted to look nice.

The thing was that she had not tried to put on make-up since she hurt her wrist, so this could be fun.

Taking it slowly and using both hands, she was able to get some mascara and eye shadow on without it looking too bad.  At least looking at herself in the mirror, it made her feel better.  Since they were going so early to the movie and having popcorn and sugar, with no dinner, she decided to have a couple of sausages before she went.

Just before it was time to leave, she put on her jeans and an avocado green silk shirt.  It was a drive in movie, so not too dressy but she wanted to look nice.

Charlie showed up right at 5:30.  As they walked to the car, he told her he had almost forgotten about dinner so he had stopped at Subway and bought her the same thing she had on Wednesday.  He hoped that was ok.

She giggled. "That's fine.  That was very nice of you." So much for the sausage she had.  Now she had to pretend she was hungry.

He drove towards the ball park and they stopped at the convenience store right outside of the park.  He asked if she felt ok to walk in or if she just wanted him to get her something.  She was glad he asked, she really didn't feel like walking in.  She had him get her a Dr. Pepper and some caramel M & M's.  He came back with an extra-large soda and a family size bag of M & M's.

She laughed, embarrassed.  "I didn't need a bag that large."

"I figured you could have some for later."

When they go to the ballpark, he showed them his ticket on his phone and they had him pull up in the middle since his vehicle was kind of large.  They put the smaller cars in the front.  Charlie set the radio to the local station so they would get sound, then he reached back and brought the sandwiches into the front seat so they could eat.  He handed Sara hers after taking it out and wrapping the paper around it so it was easier for her to handle it with her bad hand.

"Thank you," she blushed.  "Sometimes I feel so useless."

"You're not useless, you just have an injury.  It will get better."

He smiled at her.

They ate their sandwiches in silence.

When they were almost done eating, he let her know about the popcorn.  He pulled the huge bag of Harkins popcorn into the front seat.  He had paper cups for the popcorn and he filled one and handed it to Sara.  They talked and ate popcorn until the movie started.

Sara had enjoyed the talk before the movie.  They were both about the same age, so they remembered when real drive-in movies were the thing.  She talked about how they would put on their pajamas and pile into the station wagon to go to the drive-in.  They would usually fall asleep before the movie was over and so then mom and dad would carry them into the house when they got home.  She even shared how they would pretend to be asleep since if they were found awake, they had to walk into the house.  If they were asleep, Mom or Dad would carry them in.

Charlie's experience had been much the same, except that sometimes they had taken his cousins with them.  It had been a little crowded with the four of them in the back of the station wagon.  He remembered it being a lot of fun though.

The movie was enjoyable and it had been nice to get out and do something.  Sara had been cooped up for so long she really had a good time.

When they got back to her place, he walked her to the door, carrying her big bag of M&M's and water. She just had to maneuver the cane.  At the door he paused, then said, "I would like to kiss you but since we are technically quarantined, I'm going to skip it tonight.  Maybe after 14 days, if neither one of us is sick, we can kiss then."

 Sara giggled, "I'm going to hold you to that."

He held up his fingers, "Scouts honor."

"Were you even a scout?"

"Yes, I was," he acted hurt that she would even doubt him.

"Sara laughed.

Charlie took her keys and unlocked the door before opening it and letting her in.  She leaned back against the door after she closed it behind her and thought about what it would be like kissing Charlie. She had thought about it before but since he brought it up, she couldn't help dreaming about it. She had really enjoyed the evening.  She kind of liked Charlie.

# Chapter 7

The next couple of weeks were fun.  Charlie picked Sara up every day for physical therapy and they had lunch either before or after.   On Friday, at the end of the second week, Charlie had asked her if she wanted to take a drive up in the mountains the next day.  It would be something fun to get her out of the house and it was a little cooler up in the mountains than it was in Phoenix.

Sara had eagerly agreed.

"What a great idea," she said.

Charlie picked her up at eight and they stopped for breakfast at Jack in the Box.  They headed out of Phoenix on highway 89 A.  Sara looked out the window at the sage brush and the sand.  Many people saw the Arizona landscape as dull and boring but Sara had grown up here and had learned to love it.  There was still something calming about driving out through the desert, getting out of the city.  She did love the sand and the sage brush and the cacti.  Majestic saguaros dotted the landscape with their many arms reaching up to the sky.  Saguaros developed arms when they were damaged, developing an arm to cover up the hole.  She looked at all the other cacti along the side of the road, the jumping cactus, century plants.  Sometimes you actually saw a century plan in bloom which only happened once in a century.  It was all beautiful to her.  As they got further out of the city there were the flat topped mountains called buttes that Arizona was known for.  Sara sat back to relax and enjoy the ride.

At first, they were both quiet and just enjoyed the landscape but then Sara started asking questions about his life and his family.

"Do you only have one sister or are there other siblings?"

"No just one sister.  She is also a lot younger, but she's a good sister and we have some great times."

"How about you?  I don't know if you have ever mentioned siblings."

"I have a brother and a sister.  Both younger."

"Do you see them often?"

"I see my sister Darla a lot and talk to her on the phone but Oliver lives in New York, so he's a little more difficult to see.  Haven't seen him or his family for a few years."

"I'm sorry.  Do you miss him?"

"Yes, but he was kind of distant right after he graduated from high school, then he took off to New York.  Didn't really want to keep in touch.  Not sure why."

"What about your parents?"

"Both of my parents are gone," she sighed. "Mom went first from cancer, then Dad followed soon after, he just couldn't survive without her."

"Sorry,"

"What about your parents?"

"My mom is still here.  Dad died a few years ago after a stroke.  It was kind of a good thing he didn't stick around; he had no quality of life and would have just been a burden on mom.  Mom is doing well and even has a new boyfriend at eighty-two."

"That's great." Sara laughed.

"What about your husband?" Charlie asked.  He was afraid to ask but felt like their relationship was getting to the point that they talk about him.

"Well, we met our first year of college.  We got married when I was twenty and started a family right away.  Things were good but we got lost in the daily survival of kids and family and paying bills.  He was a computer nerd.  Spent long hours at work and even when he wasn't working, spent a lot of time at home on the computer.  He was an okay provider and we had what we needed until he passed.  Since he had just paid everything and didn't bother me with the details, that's when I figured out, we had nothing.  I had to sell the house because I couldn't make the house payment.  It broke my heart because there were so many memories there.  The kids had grown up there.  My best friend in the whole world lived next door and I had to leave all of that behind."

Charlie looked over at her.  Her gaze was off in the distance as she remembered.  There were tears in her eyes.

"Sorry, I didn't mean to make you feel bad."

She shook it off and said, "No, that's ok.  It's time I get past it."

He put his hand on her knee.  He could feel the electricity between them.  She didn't move away though.

"It's ok to be sad.  You have been through a lot in just a few years.  I wasn't trying to do anything but be your friend."

She smiled and patted his arm.  "I know and I appreciate it.  I have had a great time the last few weeks.  You have made me feel better."

She leaned back in her seat and looked back at him.  "So, why are you not married?"

He looked towards the side window.  "Her name was Wendy and she died of cancer.  We didn't find out until after we were engaged and she didn't last long.  It was too late when they found it."

Tears came to his eyes and he struggled not to cry. He finished.  "I thought she was the only one for me and I was devastated for years.  I guess I had put her on such a pedestal that no one else was as good as she was.  I now realize that our love story had just started and who knows where it would have ended up if she had lived."

He looked over at Sara and put his hand on her knee again.  "You, however, have changed that for me.  I guess I feel like you might be different."

Sara felt a twinge in her heart.  She felt for the man, but she was glad he was changing his opinion. She felt the same way about him but didn't want to end up with a broken heart if he couldn't make any sort of commitment.  Maybe he just needed time. She could still enjoy the friendship.

As they got closer to Jerome, you could see the red rocks of Sedona, and the San Francisco Peaks. Jerome was an old copper mine ghost town, built on the side of Cleopatra hill.

Charlie stopped at the local information bureau to find things for them to do.   They decided to go see the Gold king mine museum and ghost town.  They had waited for a while to actually go into the museum.  The museum was spacing out how often they let people enter.  You had to follow the tour and the tour groups were small.  Luckily there was a place for Sara to sit while they waited.  After touring the museum and ghost town, they found a little café for lunch.  The café was small, so they took their sandwiches to go and Charlie opened the back of the SUV and they sat there to eat.

. After lunch Sara asked if they could go check out the gift shops.  She loved to look in gift shops when visiting little towns.  There were always fun things to see.  She went into the first store where she found some rocks from the mine.  Some had been made into key chains, Others were on necklaces.

Sara picked up several and looked at them.  She didn't have any money and didn't expect Charlie to buy anything but she liked to see what the local things were.  She put the rocks down and wandered on through the store looking at other things.  Charlie wandered around behind her at first, then he said he wanted to look at the knives over in the case and left her alone to look at things.

When they met up again, he had a little sack with something he purchased.  Sara thought nothing of it and they headed back to the car.

Sara was exhausted after their walk through the mine and the stores.  She settled back into the seat on the ride home and fell asleep.

# Chapter 8

Charlie drove home in silence since Sara had fallen asleep on him. She was pretty worn out from the walk around the mine. She was still healing from her accident. Maybe that had been too much for her. He thought about their conversation earlier in the day. Was he really finally getting over the loss he felt from losing Wendy? As he thought about it, he had to say yes. Yes, he was getting over Wendy. He was ready to start something new with Sara.

He looked over at her leaning against the seat with her bad hand propped up against her chest. He had asked her why she held it there so much. She had told him it was because it helped the pain to have it propped up and it also gave it some support. She still had a lot of trouble with it. He had notice she nursed it a lot. She looked beautiful sleeping with her hair draped across her face and a little smile on her face. At least she looked happy. He hoped that he could make her happy. He really felt like she needed someone to take care of her. Someone besides her son. She was right about the fact that her son shouldn't have to be responsible for his mother at such a young age. He hoped at some time to take over that role.

As Charlie got off the free-way and the traffic slowed them down, Sara started to stir.  She opened her eyes and shifted in the seat under the seat belt.

"Oh, we're almost home.  Sorry I fell asleep." She rubbed her eyes.

"That's ok, I think it was too much expecting you to traipse through the mine."

"Maybe a little.  My ankle is hurting a little."

"Sorry.  Next time we will go someplace where there is no walking."

"Next time?"  She raised her eyebrows.

"Yes, didn't you find it fun to get out of town for a change?"

"Yes, I did.  It was also much cooler."

"Well, we should do it again then shouldn't we?"

"Definitely," she decided.

Charlie pulled into the condo parking lot and parked the SUV.  He got out of the truck, slipping the bag with his purchase from the gift shop into his pocket.  He went around to the passenger side to help Sara get out.  He took the cane from the back seat then helped her step down from the passenger seat. She was so close and smelled like almonds and something else.  He wasn't sure what it was.  Then there was the messy hair from her nap that put other visions into his head of how she would look after they made love.

She was so sexy he couldn't help himself. He wrapped his arms around her waist pulling her against him and kissed her. First it was gentle.  She tasted so good.  However, he couldn't hold back.  He wanted her with every fiber of his being.  He kissed her harder, pressing his tongue between her lips.

"You are so sexy," he mumbled against her mouth.

 She smiled against his lips.  "You're sexy too."

He then reached in his pocket and pulled out the bag putting it into her hand.  She looked surprised.

He said, "Open it."  so she did.  Inside she found a necklace with a rock from the mine.

"Just a little reminder of our trip to Jerome."

There were tears in her eyes again.

"Charlie, thank you.  I will never forget.  I really had a nice time."

"So did I."  He kissed her again before he helped her into the house.

He left her sitting in the recliner saying he would call her.  He wanted to give her some time to rest since she had said her ankle was hurting.  Besides, they did have more physical therapy visits next week.

*****

Sara sat in the recliner with her ankle propped on a pillow with ice on it. She also had ice on her wrist. Charlie had gotten the ice from the freezer for her before he left.  She laid her head back against the chair with a dreaminess about her, remembering the kiss Charlie had just given her.

Her phone rang.  It was her old neighbor and best friend, Rosie.  They had lived next to each other for over twenty years.  Raised their kids together, sat many mornings having coffee and talking about everything from how to handle kids, husbands, cooking, and cleaning. Rosie had been there when she lost Robert and had helped her get through selling the house and just surviving at first.

Sara answered it cheerfully.

"You sound cheerful," Rosie said.

"Well I just had the best day."

Sara proceeded to tell Rosie about her day with Charlie.  They had talked about him right after the day he had first taken her home after physical therapy.  Rosie was excited to get more of the story.  She told her about their day, what they had talked about and how he had bought her a rock.

"A rock, like a plain old rock?"  Rosie didn't sound too excited about that.

"No, it's a rock from the mine we toured.  It's on a necklace."

"Sara took a picture of it and texted it to Rosie so she could see it.

"It's to remind me of our trip to Jerome.  I think it's kind of cute."

"Maybe if you're a penguin," Rosie laughed.

"What's a penguin got to do with it?"

Rosie explained that male penguins give their mate a pebble.

"Oh, that's kind of romantic don't you think?"
Sara cooed.

"I guess," Rosie finally agreed.

Sara then shared that he had finally kissed her.
They both screamed like a couple of school girls.

"I'm so excited for you. I have to live vicariously
through you. I'm and old married women and my
life isn't that exciting."

"Oh, that's no excuse. You and Alex love each
other. You just need to rekindle the relationship."

"True," Rosie agreed. "I wish I knew how to do
that."

After Rosie hung up, Sara thought about Charlie
and how exciting a new relationship was. Would she
and Robert have been able to make it through old age
together if he hadn't died? Well, she didn't know
and it really didn't matter since he was no longer
here. She was glad she had found Charlie. Maybe it
would be good for her to move on.

# Chapter 9

The next Friday was Charlie's last week and then his physical therapy was done.  Sara had a couple more weeks of visits.  Charlie said he was still going to come get her and drive her over for her visits.  She didn't want to put him out, even though it had been much easier for her than dealing with the insurance company cabs and she had enjoyed their lunches and talks.  In the end, Charlie said he was coming to get her, and that was that.  He told her that he had enjoyed taking her to physical therapy and he wanted to continue to help her.  "Besides," he said grinning, "I kind of like having lunch with you."

Sara smiled back, "I like having lunch with you too."

When Charlie took Sara home on Friday, he asked her to dinner for Saturday.  He knew she would be too tired on Friday, so had purposely scheduled it the next day.  He told her it would just be casual, a picnic in the park.  We will order food and sit at a table.  Just something fun to do while not being around a lot of people because of the social distancing going on.  Sara had agreed.

When Charlie picked Sara up for dinner at six on Saturday, she answered the door wearing a pink knit dress that fit her curves nicely.  Her long hair was put back in a pony tail and she was wearing make-up. He thought she looked beautiful.

At Sara's they decided to order barbecue ribs and called in the order it so they could pick it up on the way to the park.  Charlie had packed a table cloth, plates, silverware, candles, and flowers for a formal dinner.  He figured it would be fun and safer during COVID.

Charlie found a parking spot as close to a table as he could get, so Sara didn't have to walk very far.  It was next to a pond.  It took him two trips to the car to get everything to the table.  He didn't mind.  He knew that Sara couldn't walk and carry stuff with her bad hand.  Sara did take out the tablecloth and set the table while he made the second trip with the food.  It was a very pretty romantic setting for dinner.  They lit the candles and as he looked across the table at Sara, Charlie thought how beautiful she looked in the candlelight.  They had a great time talking and laughing through dinner.  Then they gathered everything up and put it back in the bags ready to go back to the car.

Charlie looked at Sara and asked her how she felt about walking around the pond a ways.  She said she thought that would be ok.  She was feeling a little better after their excursion last weekend.  Charlie noticed a bench about half way around the little pond.

"How about over to that bench?  Then we can sit and rest before you walk back."

Sara said she could walk that far, so she took Charlie's arm with her left hand and they started walking slowly towards the bench.  Charlie liked the feel of her hand looped through his arm.  She hung on a little tight since she was not using her cane and was still a little unstable on her newly healed ankle.

They finally reached the bench and Sara sat down then Charlie sat right next to her with his arm around her shoulders.  He liked sitting close to her.  He could smell her perfume and he loved the way she smelled.  They sat for a while, neither of them saying anything, just watching the ducks and other birds on the pond.  Charlie reached down and took hold of her left hand with his left hand.  She had looked at him, leaned back against him and smiled.  He had just looked into her eyes and smiled back enjoying the closeness.

They sat that way for who knows how long before Sara said she was ready to go back to the car.  They strolled slowly back to the table and Sara rested at the table while Charlie took the first load back to the car. Charlie gathered up everything else for the second load and Sara walked back to the SUV hanging on his arm.

Charlie put everything in the back of the car, then came around to open Sara's door for her.  She turned to look at him and he moved in close. Pinning her against the car.  He wrapped his arms around her waist and leaned down to kiss her. The kiss was gentle at first.  He messaged her lips with his, biting her bottom lip until she moaned.  He pressed his hands against her back, pulling her closer and pressed his tongue between her lips to explore her mouth. She tasted wonderful.  Just like the barbecue ribs they had for dinner. She wrapped her arms around his neck.  She rubbed her left hand through his hair, the right one just laid against his neck.  He felt her relax in his arms and press tighter against him.  When he finally released her lips, he looked into her eyes.  She smiled up at him.  He could see the desire in her eyes. She wanted this too.

"I really enjoy kissing you."  She grinned at him.

He grinned back, "I just find you so incredibly sexy.  I can't keep my hands off you."

She blushed. "Then please, don't stop."

He hugged her tight, "You feel so good in my arms.  Like you belong there."

Sara didn't say anything, she just leaned against his broad chest while he held her.

He held her like that for a few minutes before he let go and helped her into the car. Before he closed her door, he leaned in placing his arms on either side of her on the seat.  With his face close to hers, he looked into her eyes,

"Sexy Sara," he whispered in her ear.

She swallowed hard and blushed.   He grinned at her and closed the door.  Oh man he was hooked.  It was going to be hard to take her home after that.

# Chapter 10

Dinner at the park last night had been magical. Charlie had made the picnic at the park a formal affair with real dishes, flowers, and candlelight. He had then told her the flowers were for her and she brought them home. They looked lovely sitting on the table in the living room and made her smile every time she looked at them. They reminded her of their night at the park.

She had enjoyed dinner immensely and then he had suggested they walk over and sit on the bench at the side of the pond where they had enjoyed sitting together and watching the ducks. It was comfortable sitting there with one arm around her and holding her left hand with his left hand. She had felt safe and protected. He smelled wonderful, Polo, if she remembered right. It was all the craze for her and her friends in high school. Funny how it still made her tummy flutter just like when she was a teenager when she smelled it on Charlie. After they had walked back to the SUV where Charlie had pressed Sara up against the car and kissed her like he was a starving man. She chuckled, maybe he was.

Charlie was a good kisser and she had particularly liked the part where he told her how sexy she was.

Sara had never thought of herself that way before. She had spent so many years being a wife and mother she didn't remember the days when she was sexy. However, when Charlie looked deep into her eyes and said it, she definitely felt that way.

Sara spent the morning posting her Facebook posts and finishing up her blog.  Just as she was about to start actually writing, the phone rang.  It was Charlie.  She smiled as she answered the phone.

"Hello," her voice came out with a squeak.

"Hello, Sexy Sara," he growled.  "Just calling to see how you were.  I really enjoyed kissing you last night."  His voice was deep and a little husky.

"I enjoyed it too," she smiled to herself.

"I think you should come over for dinner on Saturday," he said.

"Dinner huh?"

"Yes, dinner and whatever else we can find to do," he said suggestively.

Sara smiled, "That sounds like fun."

"Ok, I'll be there at six"

Sara ended the call then she thought about Charlie.  Was she ready for "whatever else they could find to do?".  She definitely liked him. A lot.  Was she scared?  Definitely.  It had been years since she had sex with anyone but Robert. It made her a little nervous to think of having sex with someone new. She had to admit it was exciting too.  Maybe she just had to take it however it happened and enjoy it.

Sara spent the rest of the afternoon writing. Charlie had definitely put her in the mood for some great romance writing.  She was able to write some wonderful sex scenes while thinking about him.

About four thirty, Sara put the computer away and went out to start dinner.  She helped Robby with the cooking as much as she could since he was letting her stay there.  Robby did most of the chopping and cutting since it was difficult and not very safe for her to use a knife with her hand.  She was able to put the ingredients together and make healthy meals.  It was better that eating take out all the time which was what Robby did when she wasn't living there.

After dinner, Sara called both of her daughters to see how they were doing.  With this pandemic going around, she hadn't seen much of them or the grandchildren.  She had talked to them several times on the phone but had not said anything about Charlie. She figured she might want to start thinking about telling them.

She called Ivy first.  She was the frantic unorganized twin, while Lily was in control of everything.  Ivy flew by the seat of her pants where Lily worked off of lists.

When her daughter answered the phone, she was very frantic and the kids were screaming in the background.  Sara asked if it was a bad time.  Ivy said, "no, in fact it's a perfect time, I need a break. She held the phone away while she asked her husband to watch the kids while she talked to her mom, then she came back.

Ivy said, "how is it that you always know when to call?"  I've had a horrible day and I really need to talk with my mom."

Sara laughed.  "I guess it's just mother's intuition. You have a fifty-fifty chance that I will call either you or Lily."

"Well, I'm glad you called me right this second before I killed someone," she said.

"It has been chaos with Jimmy working from home and all of the kids here. I'm about to go psycho. I can't get anything done."

"So tell me about it."

Ivy proceeded to tell her about how after breakfast she had all the kids sit down at the table with paints, to paint pictures. Well, they started making comments about each other's pictures and soon they were fighting and painting on the other person picture to ruin it. She had been trying to vacuum the living room which she hadn't been able to do for two days because of their stuff everywhere. When she turned off the vacuum and heard them fighting, she went back to the kitchen to find paint everywhere on the table, their clothes, and the floor. She was so mad, she just grabbed everything off the table and threw it in the trash. Then they started whining about the paint. She told them it was over, no more paint. Then she sent them all to take baths and get on clean clothes. She had the clothes soaking in the kitchen sink, but she wasn't sure if she could get the paint out. She might be throwing those out too. Jimmy was in his office working with the door closed and a sign that said "keep out" taped to the door. He said he heard the fracas but he had work to do.

She said, "mom, I know he has work to do but so do I and it is much harder to keep the house clean with everyone here 24/7.  I can't get anything done."

Sara said, "I know it's hard but maybe you shouldn't worry so much about the housework with everyone stuck at home.  Find some fun family activities and worry about the rest when we can all get back to our regular activities."

"I know," Ivy said.  "I just don't want the housework to get out of control."

"Sounds like it already is," Sara said.  "It will be much easier to get caught up when the kids can go out and play and have activities again though."

Ivy sighed, "maybe your right, she said.  I'll load them all in the car and take them for a drive.  Maybe we can see something interesting and that will at least get them out of the house for a while."

"Good idea," Sara said.  Ivy was always her frantic child where everything had to be perfect.  Her twin sister Lily was more levelheaded and a little more laid back.  How that happened when they were identical twins, she didn't know but it had always been like that.

With Ivy calmed down, she said, "Well, I will let you go.  I just wanted to check in.  Have fun."

"We will, thanks Mom, Ivy said.

After she hung up with Ivy, she called Lily.  Lily of course had everything under control.  She had made everyone get up early and run circles around the park.  There was literally nobody there so they had it all to themselves.  Now the kids were playing video games or reading quietly in their rooms.

"You need to call and have a talk with your sister this evening.  She needs a little help in trying to control her brood.  They are going for a drive right now, but she has had quite the day and could use some pointers."

Lily said, "ok, I will.  We haven't talked in a while anyway, so I should call."

"So, Mom, how are you doing?" she asked.

"I'm doing ok", she said.  "I got my website up and running and connected my Facebook page. I've posted a few times there and I am getting followers."

"That's great," she said.  "I'm glad you are finding something that interests you and hopefully things will work out so you can make some money too.”

“Yeah, that would sure be nice,” Sara said.

“How’s Robby doing?” Lily asked

“He’s doing ok,” Sara said. “He has locked himself in his office and I don’t hear much all day. He’s a lot like your dad in that respect. We do have dinner together a lot and talk and that is nice.”

“Good, I’m glad you’re not spending all of your time alone.” Said Lily.

Sara almost told her about Charlie, but then decided against it.

“Well, I will let you go, Lily, I just wanted to make sure you were ok.” Sara said.

“We are doing ok Mom, although it isn’t easy with everyone at home, we will survive.” Lily said.

# Chapter 11

Charlie had just gotten off the phone with Sara when his sister Gretchen called.

"What have you been up to lately, we haven't seen you for a while?"

"I've been busy.  Just trying to catch up from my shoulder surgery."

"How is your shoulder?"

"It's fine.  Hardly hurts anymore."

"Are you still doing physical therapy?"

"No, that was over a couple of weeks ago."

"How are you doing with all this COVID stuff?"

"I'm ok.  Try not to listen too much to the news and keeping busy helps."

"Are you getting tired hanging out all alone?"

Charlie Chuckled.  "Haven't been exactly alone.  I met someone at physical therapy."

"Wow," she said.  "it's been a while hasn't it?"

"Don't give me any grief.  It has been a while, but I'm thinking this one might be different."

"Different how?"

"I am really enjoying her company and she makes me forget about Wendy and I concentrate more on her."

"So, how does dating work in the middle of a pandemic?"

"Well, I gave her a ride to physical therapy for two weeks and we've been out a few times before I actually kissed her."

"So, two weeks quarantine?" she laughed.

Then she said, "I'm glad you are finally letting go. I know you loved Wendy, but that was a long time ago and I was worried you had put her on such a high pedestal that you would never find anyone that measured up."

"I think that might have been the case, but something about Sara is different."

"How about coming over for dinner and telling us about her?  Evie and Eddie would be glad to see you and Ed I'm sure would like to hear about Sara.  He worries about you too."

"Ok, I will do that."

They agreed on Monday night.

When Charlie showed up Monday night, Evie and Eddie were glad to see him.  He always brought them something, tonight it was candy.

Gretchen made them put the candy next to their plates to eat after dinner then they went to help her set the table.

Ed came out of his office just as they ran off.  He slapped Charlie on the back, "How are you doing old man?  Heard you have a new girlfriend."

"Yeah, I met her at physical therapy.  It started out as just a ride to and from therapy because she had an accident and can't drive.  Her insurance would pay for a cab, but they were not getting her back and forth very good.  I thought she was cute, so I offered her a ride.  After taking her back and forth a couple of times and to lunch, I decided I liked her."

Ed wrapped his arm around Charlie's back and said,

"It is about time you found yourself a girl.  I thought we had lost you to bachelorhood." He laughed.

"They headed toward the dining room where Gretchen was filling the water glasses and the kids were bringing in the food.  She had made her spinach stuffed pork chops which were Charlie's favorite and carrots, potatoes, and salad.

They all sat down and the table and the kids started telling him about how they were talking with their friends on the computer since they were not able to get together and play.  They also told him about the art activities Gretchen had them doing.  Gretchen was a big crafter and had a whole room full of supplies.  They seemed to really be enjoying themselves.

After dessert, chocolate cake, which was also Charlie's favorite, Eddie went off to play chess with a friend and Evie was going to go play with her dolls. That left just the adults to talk about Charlies love life.

Charlie told them about seeing Sara at physical therapy, then the next time finding her waiting for over an hour for her cab.  He had given her a ride home that day and taken her to lunch on the way home.  They had so much fun talking that he had decided to drive her to and from physical therapy all the time.  He told them about the lunches before and after and how they kind of waited to make sure neither of them had COVID before actually kissing.

It seemed a little weird talking with Ed and Gretchen about someone other than Wendy.  He hadn't talked about any of the other women he dated with them.  He could already tell though that Sara was different.  Sexy Sara was definitely changing his life for the better.

Gretchen was all excited.  She had often complained about not having a sister in law.  She had missed out on not having a sister and then when Charlie never got married, she felt gypped there too.

"So, when do we get to meet her.  We can have dinner next weekend if you want."

Charlie laughed, "Give us some time, will you?  I think it's a little early to start throwing her to the wolves."

"I'm not a wolf but ok, I'll try to be patient.  It's just you have never even talked about the other women you dated."

"That's because I never went out with anyone more than once or twice.  At least give us a couple of weeks"

Later when leaving, Charlie assured Gretchen that they would be able to meet her soon.

# Chapter 12

On Saturday, Sara spent the morning getting her daily tasks done with her business.  She had Facebook posts to set up and recipe's to find.  After lunch she got in the shower, then she worked on the blog while her hair dried.  It had started out fairly short in January, but with the time spent in the rehab facility and now the couple of months with quarantine, it was feeling a little long and shaggy.  She decided at the last minute to trim a little off.  She gripped the scissors in her right hand as best she could, leaned upside down brushing all the hair to the front, then taking a little off the ends.  She knew it would be shaggy but with her long hair it wouldn't show much and it would take some weight off the length.  It felt better immediately. She then put a little conditioner on the ends and rubbed gel all over fluffing it so it would curl. Luckily, her hair was getting more natural curl as she got older.

At half past four, she brushed out her hair, put on some make-up and decided what to wear.  She wanted something comfortable, but kind of sexy since, they both knew where this evening was going.  She was a little nervous since this was her first real relationship since her husband passed away.  She was feeling pretty comfortable around Charlie and enjoyed their time together, but he had really upped the ante during their date at the park.  It was exciting that he felt that way about her, but still made her nervous.  She decided on a pair of light green colored jeans and a fitted tank top in black.  It was comfortable, yet sexy and showed off her curves.  She added a gold necklace and gold earrings.  She wore her hair down.  With the half inch taken off, it was a little bouncier and curled nice.  She sprayed on a little perfume then added some colored lip gloss.  She smiled at herself in the mirror.  She felt pretty for a change.

Right at six the doorbell rang.  She went to get the door.

There stood Charlie in a tan button down shirt with the sleeves folded up to his elbows.  He wore dark brown dress pants and looked very sexy himself.  She stepped back and let him in.  He took her in his arms and gave her a kiss.  When he released her lips, she just looked into his eyes and said, "Hi," with a cute little smile.  He grinned and said hi back.  He also smelled incredible.  A little polo and a bit of manliness.

"Let me get my stuff and I'll be ready. I hope you don't mind if I bring a few extra things, just in case."

"Not at all," he smiled. "Bring whatever you want. Better to be prepared." He winked.

She blushed.

Charlie took her bag as they walked out to his SUV. He walked slowly next to her as she maneuvered with the cane. He touched her back with his hand and whispered in her ear that he was kind of hoping she would spend the night, so he was glad she had planned ahead. His touch on her back sent shivers through her body. He put her bag in the back seat and then helped her into the front seat. As he climbed in on his side, he looked at her and grinned.

"We are going to have a good time tonight."

She blushed.

When they got to Charlies house, he pulled into the driveway and stopped long enough to open the garage door with the remote.

Sara looked at his house. It was a nice house. Tan with dark green trim and shutters. The lawn was neatly cut and trimmed. He had a nice cactus garden in the center of the lawn.  Charlie opened the garage and drove in, shutting the door behind them.  He then came around the car, taking her bag and cane out of the back seat, then helped her out of the car before they went in the back door of the house.

Charlie put her bag on the couch and closed the door behind them.  They stood in the family room.  As she looked around, it was very cozy looking.  Soft couches and chairs and a couple of quilts laying on the back of the couch.  Sara just kind of stood there, not knowing really what to do, but it didn't take Charlie long.  He stepped up next to her taking her in his arms and holding her chin up with his finger.  She could see the desire in his eyes.

"I'm so glad you decided to come."  His voice was deep and gravely.

"I'm glad too," but the sound barely came out.

He reached down, taking the hold of the hem of her tank top, and pulling it up over her head being careful with her sore hand.  She was wearing a black lace bra.

"ooh, Sexy," he said as he reached out and took hold of her breast with his hand.  As he touched her breast through the lace, her nipples turned to points.

His touch sent sensations through her whole body, straight to her core.  She grabbed hold of his shoulders with her hands as he continued to rub his thumb over her nipple.  She let out a small groan as his thumb brought her nipple to a hard ball.  Their eyes were locked.  He reached around the back and undid her bra, dropping it on the floor next to them.

Sara felt a little embarrassed standing there half naked in front of him.  Would he like what he saw?  She suddenly felt old and not so sexy.  However, Charlie still looked at her with desire in his eyes.

"Beautiful," was all he said as he raked his eyes over her body before wrapping his arms around her again and looking into her eyes.  He whispered in her ear,

"Do you know how sexy and beautiful you are?"

She didn't know how to answer.  She really didn't know, although Charlie was making her feel very sexy.  Luckily, he didn't wait for an answer.

"Here let me show you."

He started nibbling on her ear and licking her neck with his tongue.  She could feel her breasts tighten as they were pressed against his shirt. It felt so good that she started to melt in his arms and her knees got weak. She wrapped her arms around his neck so she didn't fall. He held on tighter, holding her up while he continued to nibble on her ear and he started rubbing her back. She lost all ability to breathe and when she tried to talk, it just came out in a moan,

"Ugh," he grunted. "Do you know what that does to me?"

Without letting go, he led her back to the bedroom where he undid the button on her pants and slid them down around her ankles along with her panties. He had her sit on the edge of the bed where he pulled them off. He took off his shirt and pants so he stood naked before her. He was a good looking man for being sixty. He instructed her to scoot back on the bed, then he lay down beside her, making sure he was on her left side and he wasn't bothering her hand. She was grateful he was being careful.

"I don't want to hurt your hand," he whispered as he looked into her eyes.

Just be gentle and don't try to hold my hands down. I will cooperate with whatever you want, just don't touch my wrist."

"Whatever I want?" he mused.

She giggled. "Within reason."

Being careful not to touch her sore wrist he began to kiss and tease her again.

He took her breast in his mouth and the sensations that ran through her body were exquisite. Her breath quickened and her body was all tingly.

He whispered, "I can tell you like that. You are so beautiful when you react to my touch."

She opened her eyes to look into his. His eyes were dark and the pupils large. She reached up putting her hand on his cheek and kissed his lips. He returned the kiss with eagerness and he ran his hand down her side. She pressed her hips up, wanting to be closer.

Charlie just chuckled.

He moved his hand from her hip to rub his thumb against her mound, finding her clit. She was having a hard time holding still. His touch caused a fire to burn between her legs. He slipped a finger inside her. She was so ready to come, she could feel herself starting to lose control. She closed her eyes again and lay her head back on the bed. She moaned loudly as the sensations took hold and she let go. Her

orgasm took over and she felt the fire burn through
her reaching every part of her body.

Charlie held her close until she came down. She
heard him say, "Baby that was beautiful to watch."

She opened her eyes and looked at him. With a
sparkle in her eyes she smiled, "that was wonderful."
She reached up and kissed him.

He held her in his arms and started kissing her
again. She felt her body start to automatically
respond again and it wasn't long until she was feeling
the second orgasm coming.

This time he massaged her breasts until she was
squirming again, then he tested her opening to see
how wet she was.

"You are nice and wet," he said. He spread her
legs out and moved between them before directing
his member into her opening. He pushed gently at
first, then deeper and deeper until he was all the way
in.

"Oh my God, Charlie, you feel so good." She
breathed.

Charlie just groaned.

He started moving in and out slowly.  So slowly she could hardly stand it.  She looked into his eyes and tried to speak but it just came out as a moan. She raised her hips to meet him, trying to make him go faster but he was not to be hurried.  He just chuckled. As she looked at him, she could tell he was watching her, checking her reaction to every move he made. She couldn't talk, she could barely breathe.  He smiled and then started pressing harder and faster until she thought she was going to die.  She shuddered as she hit the second climax then Charlie pressed one last time, hard and deep before groaning and spilling into her. He collapsed on top of her.  She didn't mind.  She enjoyed the closeness and the feel of his chest against her breasts.

As she started to regain strength the wrapped her arms around his neck and rubbed the nape of his neck with her hands.  He groaned deep in his chest but didn't move.

They lay together for a while until the sun was almost gone and the room was starting to get dark. Charlie rolled over on his side, resting his hand on her hip.

"So, are you hungry yet?" he asked as he gently rubbed her bottom.

She hadn't thought much about it but now that he mentioned it, she realized she was starving.

"I'm famished." She said.

With that, he got up, put on his shorts then helped her up off the bed. She put on her underwear and Charlie handed her one of his shirts to put on. She held it up to her face. It smelled like Charlie.

While she was dressing, he headed out to heat up the barbecue. When he came back in, two minutes later, she was standing in the kitchen. He asked if she wanted some wine.

"I would love some."

He poured them both a glass before taking the ribs out of the fridge and then he suggested that she bring the wine glasses and come out to the patio while he grilled the ribs.

Sara sat at the table and talked with Charlie while he grilled. It was a nice evening and he had a beautiful back yard. Raised beds along the fence with all kinds of plants and vines. He even had a fish pond over at one side of the patio. Sara had to walk over to look at the fish. It was all so serene and peaceful. The back yard was walled off, so it was very private and she didn't feel embarrassed to wander around with only her panties and Charlies shirt.

When the ribs were done, they took them back inside where he had salad to go with them. They ate inside because it was summer in Arizona so too hot to eat outside. After dinner, Charlie refilled the wine glasses and they took them into the family room, just off the kitchen to sit and talk.

Sara sat on the end of the couch and placed her wine glass on the table next to her. Charlie sat next to her placing his glass on the coffee table in front of them. He wrapped his arms around her. She leaned her head against his chest.

"There, that is much better," he whispered in her ear.

"Hmmm," she moaned.

Charlie took his finger and lifted her chin up towards him. He looked into her eyes and she could see the desire as he looked at her. He reached down, taking her lips with his and gently kissing her. As he nibbled and tasted her lips, she let out another moan.

"That really turns me on when you do that." He said as he moved his hand down to her breast where he started to palm it through the shirt fabric.

"Oh, Charlie,"

"You like that?"

"Yes," she moaned as she placed her hand up alongside his cheek. "I love that."

He undid the buttons on the shirt until he could reach inside to touch her breast. He began to massage the tip of one breast. She let out another moan.

She twisted to the side, so she could lay back against the arm of the couch and lifted her legs up to rest on Charlie's lap. Charlie grabbed hold of the shirt sleeves and pulled so her arms came out. She was now laying there in just her panties.

"Lovely," he said as he leaned down and took her breast in his mouth.

She took hold of the back of his head with her left hand, holding him close as he licked and sucked her breast. She was touching his head with her right hand but was careful so as not to hurt it. She could feel the flutter start between her legs. She would have thought by this time her body was too tired, but it sprung to life again. She started to squirm as he took hold of the other breast with his mouth.

"Oh, baby, you taste so good,"

He moved his hand down to her hip and began to massage her butt.  She was getting really excited now and could hardly hold still.  He traced his finger under the edge of her panties.

"Oh, Charlie," she cooed.

He slid his finger down to the slick wet opening underneath.  He started to massage her clit with his thumb.  She was now so excited she could not hold still.

"Oh, Charlie," she called out as she arched toward him.

"I know sweetheart, just relax and enjoy it,"

He continued to massage and tantalize her.

It wasn't long until she was bucking involuntarily and he was smiling, enjoying the show.

"Cum for me sweetheart,"

She laid her head back against the cushion as the waves of her orgasm washed over her.  As she came down and started to relax, Charlie took her in his arms and held her close.

"Baby, that was beautiful.  I love to watch you."

She wrapped her arms around his strong torso and settled in against his chest.  She loved the feeling of being so close to him.  She didn't remember feeling like this before.  At least not for a very long time.

They sat holding each other sipping wine and not saying much.  Finally, their wine glasses empty, Charlie stood up, pulling her up off the couch with one hand, he grabbed her bag with his other hand and led her into the bedroom where he dropped her bag on a chair and led her over to the bed.  He pulled the covers back, letting her climb in and scoot over before climbing in next to her.  He wrapped his arms around her again and with her head against his chest, they curled up together.

Charlie kissed her on the head, "Sara, I haven't felt like this for a long time.  Something about you is different."

"I'm enjoying this so much," she said.  "I'm feeling like it's different too."

She loved being so close.  It wasn't long until they were both asleep.

# Chapter 13

Charlie woke up Sunday morning to sunlight shining in the window and a sexy little woman curled up next to him. He had been thrilled that she agreed to come to dinner and he planned on making it a wonderful evening for her. He had never dreamed it would turn out like it did. There was just something about her that was different. More like what he had felt for Wendy, his fiancé who had died from cancer. It had been quite a few years, but he had not been able to let go until now. Why was Sara different? He didn't know but she was.

He watched her sleep for a minute. So peaceful and beautiful with her messed up hair. He climbed out of bed and went to the bathroom. When he came back, she was awake.

"Hey beautiful, how are you?"

She tried to move, then groaned.

"I'm so stiff," she grumbled.

"Sorry. Maybe we overdid it a little."

"Oh, I definitely think we overdid it." she laughed

"I'll try to be easier on you until we get you into shape." He grinned.

She rolled out of bed and stumbled into the bathroom, stretching, and moaning all the way.

When she came back out, he said, "Why don't you take a nice hot shower then I will massage your sore muscles with some lotion?"

 She eyed him suspiciously, "Ok, but no funny stuff.  I need to be able to move again."

He smiled and held up his two fingers again. "Scouts honor,"

He kept his promise and after the shower and the massage, she was feeling a little better.  Sara got dressed and then Charlie took her to breakfast.  He couldn't help but smile at her.  He had enjoyed what they shared and he still hadn't had enough.  He found her very sexy.  He also liked how she blushed when he called her Sexy Sara.

As he stood on the porch after walking her to the door, he took her in his arms, kissed her again and made her promise to come stay again the next weekend.

"I promise to be less aggressive. Although you do bring out the wild man in me."

"I do love spending time with you and I really enjoyed making love, but maybe we should do more cuddling and talking until my body gets used to this."

"Sounds good. I do want you to enjoy it and not hate me afterward."

"Oh, I could never hate you. You make me feel wonderful."

# Chapter 14

Charlie called Sara several times during the next week but they didn't get together until Saturday morning.  Charlie had suggested another drive through the mountains then to stay with him that night.

Sara was excited for another fun trip with Charlie.  Life was very boring with everyone in quarantine and so many places shut down, there wasn't a lot to do.  Sara's ankle was still healing and she was tired of sitting around.  She couldn't do much walking or hiking, so the next best thing was driving.

He picked her up early, before sunrise this time and they stopped for breakfast again.  As he drove through the desert towards the mountains, they watched the sun come up.  It was breath taking.

Sara sat back quietly looking around.  This time they headed out US 60 through Miami and Globe and further up in the mountains.  The scenery was beautiful at first as they headed out through Mesa and Apache Junction. They drove past the Superstition mountains which was a beautiful sight, then they hit the Miami-Globe area.  They were also old mining towns but were very ugly dirty places.  Then they headed up towards the white mountains.

Sara sat back in the seat, just watching the scenery, and thinking about other times she had been out here, traveling with Robert and the kids.  There were some great memories there.

"Penny for your thoughts,"

She looked at him and smiled.

"I'm glad you thought of these little day trips out to see nature."

"Good.  I think getting out in nature is always relaxing."

"So where are we going?"

"That is a surprise," he smiled mischievously.

"I thought we would drive until lunch.  I know just the spot to stop."

"I love surprises." she said as she took a drink of her soda and settled back against the seat.  They talked about places they had been, trips they had taken with their families.

The terrain changed from ugly sandy desert to lush green forests.  The pine trees stood tall and majestic, the oak trees spread their limbs high and far.  There were small bushes and wildflowers along the side of the road.  This part of Arizona was beautiful.

About 11:30, Charlie pulled into Show Low.  Show Low had kind of an interesting story.  It was named after a card game held between two ranchers where during a card game called Seven up, one of the ranchers told the other that if his card showed low, he would take the ranch.  The main street in Show Low is called the Deuce of Clubs because it is the lowest card in the deck.

Charlie pulled up to the Show Low café before turning to look at Sara.

She was smiling, "What a wonderful surprise."

Charlie winked, "I thought you might like it."

He climbed out and went around to open her door and help her out.  Sara had a roast beef sandwich and coleslaw.  Charlie ordered meatloaf and mashed potatoes and gravy.  They again took their order to go then ate in the back of the SUV.

After lunch when they were back in the car, Sara asked, "So, what now?"

"Well, I thought since we were already here, we could find someplace to stay tonight and then go back tomorrow."

Sara smiled.  "I think it's a great idea.  Did you plan this? Is that why you suggested bringing my things and staying the night at your place?"

Charlie grinned sheepishly, "You caught me."

They found a hotel and checked in, then Charlie brought everything into the room.

Sara was sitting on the edge of the bed when he came in with the bags and her extra pillows.  It was all Sara could do to get herself into the room with her bad ankle.

Charlie dumped the bags on the chair and threw the pillows on the bed before pulling Sara to her feet and wrapping his arms around her.

"Here we are Sexy Sara, and nothing to do," he growled into her ear.

"Like you hadn't already thought of that," she smiled at him and her eyes shown.

He started rubbing his hand up and down her back. "How about a little fun in the afternoon?"

Sara blushed thinking about what he meant by that. She whispered. "Sounds good," as she wrapped her arms around his neck, pressing her breasts against him.

Charlie started kissing her. His kisses were deep and sensuous and intense. Their tongues were tangled as he pressed into her mouth. It wasn't long until she couldn't breathe and she wasn't sure she could stand up anymore. Charlie took her top off and undid her bra letting it fall to the floor. He then undid her pants and let them fall to the ground around her ankles. Then he pushed her panties down as well. She grabbed hold of his arms to steady herself while she stepped out of them.

Charlie lay her back on the bed then he removed his shorts and his shirt. He smiled down at her as she spread her legs willingly for him to kneel between them. He lifted her hips and positioned himself so that he could press into her opening. He started gentle at first. Pressing little by little allowing her to relax around him as he massaged her clit. Little by little he pushed further in until he completely filled her. She could feel her body relax around him and start to squeeze automatically.

"Oh, sweetheart, that feels so nice when you do that."

She smiled and continued to watch his face as he started to move in and out and her body continued to pulsate around him. What a wonderful feeling. As he got more and more excited, he started to move faster and faster. Pretty soon they were both breathing heavily and Sara thought she was going to pass out. She closed her eyes as the waves of orgasm washed over her. She couldn't believe the feelings this man could instill in her. Charlie reached his release shortly after, spilling into her before collapsing on top of her. As they both lay there catching their breath, she wrapped her arms around his head, holding him against her chest and savoring the feelings of closeness she felt with Charlie. She hadn't felt this good in a very long time.

They lay, naked bodies entwined until the sun went down and the shadows settled in. Charlie rolled off of her and asked if she was ready for dinner. She felt like she was starving again. It seemed like lunch had been so long ago. Of course they had also spent a lot of energy making love.

"Yes, I'm about to die.  I don't know how you always tend to distract me from eating."

"Some things are way more fun," he grinned.

They decided to order delivery so they didn't have to get dressed again.  They sat on the bed to eat.  Sara in Charlie's shirt and panties and Charlie in just shorts.

They didn't talk much as they ate.  It seemed that they didn't need to say anything.  They had shared some great experiences and that seemed enough right now.

# Chapter 15

It had been a wonderful day with Charlie, driving through the mountains.  Having lunch at café and finding a hotel for a little afternoon sex.  Sara really liked Charlie and it seemed to her that he liked her as well.  He was a very attentive lover and she felt things with him she had never felt before.  Maybe she had lost something with Robert.  They had gotten lost in raising kids and paying bills. She also felt very comfortable with Charlie.  Comfortable enough to sit in her underwear while they ate dinner on the bed in the hotel.

After dinner, Sara decided she needed a shower.  She felt kind of sweaty and sticky after making love and she needed to wash that off before bed.

"I think I'll take a shower," she said as she headed towards the bathroom.

Charlie waited just long enough for her to get the warm water running when he stuck his head in.

"Mind if I join you," he grinned at her sheepishly.

Sara giggled.  "You were never going to let me shower alone, were you?"

"I thought I could help with all the places you can't reach."  He chortled.

"Come on in," she laughed.

He stepped into the shower, taking her in his arms again and kissing her passionately.  He then turned her around and soaped up her back and then reached around to the front, soaping up her breasts and belly. She had laid her head back against his chest and as he spread the soap further down her body towards her soft mound, she moaned.

"Baby," he grunted in her ear.  "That sound so turns me on."

Sara could feel him getting hard against her back.

"It feels so good," she mumbled.

Charlie wrapped his arm around her waist to hold her up while he continued to massage her mound. Her legs felt weak and she started to melt against him.  The sensations were mind numbing.  She felt his finger against her clit.  She lifted her knees and clenched her thighs together, trying to hold Charlie's hand against her, then the feelings washed over her as she collapsed in his arms.

Charlie stopped pressing her clit and wrapped both arms around her until she could stand again. She twisted in his arms, wrapping her arms around his neck, and pressing her breasts against his chest. He groaned at the feel of her body pressed tightly against him.  Then she reached down between them and took hold of him.  He was already stiff and ready to go.  She wrapped her fingers around him and slid her hand up and down.  Slowly and barely touching at first, then as he got more excited, she gripped harder and moved faster.  She could tell he was getting close because his breathing got more erratic and his voice got deeper.  She rubbed her thumb across the tip, several times and that was all it took before he spilled out all over.  She smiled and kissed his lips.

"I like that I can do that to you."

"I like it too." He kissed her again.

They finished washing themselves off and got out and dried off.

They curled up together in bed, exhausted but happy.

"I meant what I said before, you are different than anyone I've seen in the past."

He just wanted to be sure she understood this was not just a fling for him.

She looked up at him, placing her hurt hand gently on his cheek.  "That's nice to know."

# Chapter 16

Sunday morning they checked out of the hotel and headed back to Phoenix.  It was a nice drive.  They chatted for the first hour but it wasn't long until Sara had fallen asleep.  He had kept her pretty busy last night.  He just hoped he could stay awake long enough to drive home.

He thought about all that had happened in the last few weeks.  It had been quite a whirlwind of emotions but he did have to admit it had all been worth it.  He was falling in love with Sara.  Sexy little Sara.  Did he say love?  Yes, he was pretty sure it was love. It was kind of nice.  After losing Wendy, he never thought he would be in love with anyone else.

He started talking out loud.

"Wendy, I think I have found someone that I really care about.  I know you told me to find someone new but I have missed you so much.  I have had such a hard time getting over all the stuff we didn't get to do."

It brought tears to his eyes and he wiped them away.  It had seemed like a long time but he realized that he had to wait for Sara to be ready.  She had a family and kids to raise.  He felt bad that they hadn't been able to share that, but he was grateful to be able to spend the time with her now.

He pulled into the parking lot of her condo a couple of hours later.  As he pulled into the park, Sara woke up.  She sat up still half asleep, "Where are we?"

"We are home.  Did you have a nice nap?"

She smiled sheepishly, "Sorry, I keep falling asleep on you.  You really wore me out again this weekend."

"I know, but I just can't keep my hands off you, you are so sexy."

She reached across the console, wrapping her arms around his neck, she smiled, "It makes me feel good that you can't."

Then she whispered as if anyone else was listening, "I can't keep my hands off of you either."

He couldn't help but kiss her.  Then he got out of the truck to help her into the house with her bag and her pillows.

They walked up to the door and she found that it was locked.  She had the key but she struggled putting it in the lock with her hand.  Charlie took the key from her and helped her unlock the door.  Just as he opened the door, Robby came up from the parking lot.  Sara seemed a little embarrassed but she introduced them.  Robby was a very nice looking man and he smiled warmly at Charlie.  He didn't say anything about them being gone all weekend, but he did take Sara's bag into the house for her, leaving them to say their good byes on the step.

Charlie took Sara in his arms and looked into her eyes.

"You are so sexy," he said. "My sexy Sara."

Sara smiled and kissed him.

"You make me feel sexy."

Charlie reached into his pocket and pulled out another small bag.  Sara smiled and then looked inside.  It was another little keepsake of their trip to Show Low.  This time it was a key ring with the deuce of clubs.  Very distinct for Show Low.

"I'm going to get you something for every trip we take.  Something to always remember them by."

"That is so sweet," she had tears in her eyes again. She reached up and kissed him.

"Thank you, Charlie Chambers."

He wrapped his arms around her, holding her close and kissing the top of her head.  He really liked this woman.  More than he ever expected.

# Chapter 17

Monday morning, Sara woke to the phone ringing on the nightstand. When she picked it up, it was her sister Darla.

"Hey sis, haven't heard much from you lately."

"Yeah, I've been a little busy."

"Doing what? You have a broken wrist and ankle."

"Mostly physical therapy and a few out of town trips. Just to get out of the house."

"How have you been doing that? You have no car."

Sara finally confessed that she had met someone at physical therapy and they had been spending a lot of time together.

"Ooh, is he cute?"

"I think he's very sexy. He's big and tall and husky. We've had lunch every day when he gives me a ride to physical therapy and we've gone to the movies, to Jerome and e just got back from Show Low yesterday."

"Have you slept with him yet?"

Sara paused, "Yes."

"How was it?"

"Pretty good. Actually very good."

"Ooh," Darla squealed again.  "I'm so excited for you.  I don't want you to grow old alone.  That really worried me after Robert died."

"Well, I wasn't really worried about that, but it is nice to have someone that cares.  I am also having a lot of fun."

"Glad someone is having fun."

Sara could tell something was wrong.  Darla was usually pretty upbeat.

"What's going on?" she probed.

"Oh, I don't know.  I'm not sure."  Darla paused.

"Come on, I can tell something is wrong.  Tell me."

"I think Ralphie is cheating on me," she blurted out.

"Oh, my," Sara inhaled.

She didn't want to say so, but Ralphie was kind of a loser. He made ok money as a salesman and they had a nice house but he had the used car salesman attitude and was always trying to pull one over on someone. Sara had put up with him because Darla loved him but she never really liked him.

"So what makes you think he's cheating?"

"Well, the whole time we were quarantined together, he was always texting someone on the phone. He seemed really happy and laughing when he was texting but he seemed more insensitive and disagreeable with me. It was like he was trying to start a fight and make me throw him out. Now he is back on the road so he is gone most of the time. Last weekend he didn't even come home. He told me he had to work on Saturday and it didn't seem worth it to drive home just for Sunday then back on Monday.

The thing was that I thought I heard a woman's voice in the background when he was talking to me on the phone. Sara, I don't know what to do!"

Sara tried to remain calm. This was Darla's thing and Darla had to figure out how to handle it. Sara would have booted him out the door and let him go. In her experience if you thought something was happening it usually was.  However, he was Darla's husband and Darla needed to decide what to do.

"Well, maybe not make any rash decisions right now.  See what you can find out but I would be direct with him.  Don't follow him around and check his phone.  Ask him point blank.  Then go by his reaction.  You will know what to do then."

Darla sighed, "I know, I think I probably already know, I'm just not ready to admit it yet."

"Darla, I'm sorry.  I'm here if you need me."

After hanging up the phone Sara sat on the edge of the bed.  She felt bad for her sister.  Just another shitty thing to happen in 2020.

After talking to Darla, Sara got up, brushed her hair, and put on some shorts and a t-shirt before she went out to the kitchen for coffee then she headed back to the living room where she spent the rest of the day writing.  Her books were getting easier to write.  Not that she was actually writing about their love life, but Charlie sure did inspire her to write.  It was all working out very well.

# Chapter 18

Charlie got up early Monday morning to meet his two best friends, Dan, and Pete for a game of golf. He had taken the morning off. This was the first time he had golfed since he hurt his shoulder. It was also his first time golfing since COVID started. COVID made things a lot more complicated. You now had to wear masks in the clubhouse. The golf course had spaced the tee times further apart and the groups had to stay away from other groups while golfing. The worst part was the snack bar and the café were closed. That was too bad because after golfing, they usually stopped for lunch at the café. Even with all the changes, Charlie was glad to be back to hanging with the guys and doing what he loved.

Dan and Pete met him at the golf course. Dan was a tall, thin guy with graying blond hair. Pete was tall and big all over. Pete had played football in college. Never made it to the pros but at least it had paid for his college education. Both men were attorney's Dan was a accident attorney while Pete was a corporate lawyer. The three of them had met as undergrads in college and had maintained the friendship all these years. Dan was divorced with four kids. All of them in college. He was lucky and had been able to maintain a good relationship with the kids in spite of the problems with their mother.  Pete had never been married and had never really had a steady girlfriend either.  Charlie had been hung up on Wendy all this time and that was his excuse but Pete had never had anyone.  They hadn't talked about it much but Pete had mentioned once or twice that he just had never felt that way about anyone.

Charlie had brought his neighbor Sam with him to be the fourth person in their group.  Sam had golfed with them a lot, and fit well into the group.  Sam was a CPA and ran his tax business from his condo.  He was divorced but didn't talk much about his family.  Charlie was not sure what happened.  He knew he had a couple of kids but didn't think that they had anything to do with Sam.

As the jumped in the two rented golf carts and headed to the first hole, Charlie enjoyed the beautiful morning.  It was summer in Arizona so they had to start early to get a game in before it got too hot but he was glad to be able to get out and enjoy the day and hang out with his friends.

The three friends hadn't seen a lot of each other lately.  Mostly because Charlie had gotten hurt and had to have surgery.  Then he spent time recovering.

They made Charlie tee off first because of his shoulder injury. He missed the hole by a long shot. He definitely needed to work out with a bucket or two of balls to get his swing back.  Dan wanted to know what he'd been doing with all his time.  Charlie said,

"I just had shoulder surgery man."

 "Yes, but you had surgery how long ago and you haven't even called or anything," Pete piped up.

"I've been busy," he said, not wanting to admit having met a girl. These were his single friends and would give him quite a ribbing.

"Even sitting around the house with a bum shoulder, you could have called," Dan scolded.

"Yeah man, what are you holding out on?" Pete chided.

Sam looked at him knowingly.  He had seen him drive in with a woman in the car.  He knew she had spent the nights few times because he saw them leave the next morning when Charlie took her home.  Sam didn't say anything, of which Charlie was glad.

He paused, looking at all three men.

"I met a woman," he finally admitted.

"You mean more than a one night stand?" Pete kidded.

"Yeah.  I think I'm finally over Wendy."

"This must be some woman to make you forget about her."  Dan was flabbergasted.

"She is something. And I really like her."

He told them about meeting her at physical therapy, then giving her rides and taking her to lunch three times a week.  He told them about her accident and all the trouble she was having.  He said there was just something that drew me in even before I found out that she needed me.

"She staying over yet?" Dan waggled his eyebrows.

"A few times, and we've had a great time." Charlie boasted.

"So, what made you finally get over Wendy?" Pete enquired.

"I think I finally saw that I had put her on a pedestal and since she died, I could keep her there as the perfect woman.  Maybe nobody else had a chance.”

“Been trying to tell you that for years,” Pete added.

“I know.  Guess I’m a little slow.  It may have also taken the right woman.”

“Well,” said Dan, “sounds like we need to meet this woman.  The woman that finally caught Charlie’s attention.”

“Yeah, she’s got to be something special to turn Charlie’s head,” agreed Pete.

Sam chimed in, “She is pretty good looking and I think Charlie is a lucky man.”

“Have you met her?” Dan asked.

Sam shook his head, “No, just saw here when he brought her home a few times.”

“So, when do we get to meet her?” Pete asked.

“Maybe never,” Charlie said firmly.  “I like this woman and you guys might scare her off.”

“A little overprotective are we?” Pete jested.

"Yes I am.  She has had a hard few months and she needs someone to take care of her.  Besides, you guys get mean sometimes."

"We are mean to you bud, but we would be nice to a woman.  Especially one who would put up with you."  Dan scoffed.

As they came around to the ninth hole it was starting to get warm outside.  It was a good thing they were almost finished.  Charlie shook the front of his shirt.  He was already sweating and it wasn't past eight AM yet.  Sam patted down his forehead with a towel and took a swing.  He missed the hole by just a few feet.  Everyone else took their shot and then they finished the hole.

After golf, they headed out to a bar around the corner for sandwiches and a beer.  While they were waiting for their food, Pete stood and made a toast to Charlie and his new woman.  They all drank to it and there were a few more comments about him finally finding a woman.  Even with all the joking, Charlie was glad to get together with his friends for a while. He had missed them.

After lunch Charlie went home to relax and watch TV.  He wasn't sure what was on, just something to relax him.

He had just settled on the couch when his phone rang.  It was Gretchen.

"Hey big bro."

"Hey Gretch. what's up?"

"I've been thinking…."

Oh no, here it comes.  He hated when Gretchen had been thinking.  She was always making plans and she had this thing about trying to take care of her big brother.  He didn't know how many times she had tried to set him up with someone.  Now she had a new bone to chew on, Sara.  He just hoped she didn't get too pushy and push Sara away.

"Go ahead Grethen."

"It is time for us to meet this woman who has captured your heart.  She has to be someone special for you to jump like this."

"Ok, Gretchen, what did you have in mind?" he sighed.

"Come over next Saturday.  We will barbecue and just talk.  Nothing fancy."

"Okay, I'll check with Sara and see what she says.  No promises though."

He hung up thinking he wasn't sure if Sara was ready to meet the family yet.  Was he ready?  He wasn't sure.

# Chapter 19

It was Saturday night and they were getting ready to go to dinner at Gretchen's.  Sara had finally agreed to go after several reassurances that she would be fine.

"Gretchen likes everyone," Charlie admonished.  "She just wants to meet you."

Sara had spent Friday night at his place.  It had been another fun evening.  At least she was getting in better shape and didn't get as stiff and sore as she had the first weekend.  They had showered together this morning, then just hung around the house.  Sara had started getting ready this afternoon, putting on makeup and fixing her hair.  She had two different outfits, a knit green dress and jeans and a t-shirt with a V-neck.  She had tried both of them on but couldn't decide which one to wear.  He did like her in the green dress but that was only because it made her look so sexy.  When he had told her that and she immediately took it off.  She didn't want to be sexy around his sister.  She was now wearing the jeans and t-shirt.  She looked good in that too.  Maybe he just thought she looked good no matter what.  He smiled, even naked, she looked good.

Finally, Sara was ready to go.  He took her in his arms, kissing her.  You look fantastic baby.  Let's get going before we are late.  He helped her into the car as usual.  She was still walking with a cane but her gait seemed to be getting better.  She was doing exercises at home to strengthen her legs and ankle.  The hand was still a problem, though.

Charlie pulled into the drive at Gretchen and Ed's house.  It was the corner house in a cul-de-sac and they had a nice, neat front yard.  It was mostly rocks with a small section of grass in the middle.  Charlie liked the house.  The house itself was normal but the back yard was huge since it was the corner lot.  They had a grassy area for the kids to play, a garden and a pool off to one side.  Ed had also added an outdoor kitchen that included a nice built in grill and plenty of seating for parties.  Before COVID hit, Gretchen and Ed had thrown a lot of parties.  That was usually the place to go for holidays.  The house seemed exceptionally quiet as they walked in the door without knocking.  Charlie had never knocked at Gretchen and Ed's.  They were family.

He called out "Anybody home?" Ed stuck his head through the patio doors.

"Gretchen will be back in a few.  The kids are staying the night at grandma's house and she's just dropping them off."

"An adult only party?  We haven't had one of those in a while."

Ed finished turning the ribs on the grill and Charlie went to the fridge for a beer.  He noticed there was also wine in the fridge.  He got a wine for Sara and he grabbed a beer before he pointed her to the back yard to sit and talk with Ed.

Charlie introduced her to Ed and they started talking about Eddie and Evie and then about Sara's kids.  It was an easy conversation.

It wasn't long until Gretchen showed up.  Charlie introduced them.  Gretchen was so excited.  She told Sara that she had lost hope that Charlie would ever have a girlfriend.  With that, the two women went back in the house to make salad and talk, leaving Charlie and Ed on the patio.

Sara stood in the kitchen with Gretchen.  She had been so nervous when thinking about meeting Charlie's sister but now that she had actually met her, she wasn't so bad.  She was a lot younger and full of energy but Sara kind of liked her.  Again the topic of kids came up.  Gretchen's kids were much younger, eleven and eight.  Sara's three were grown.  They did find plenty to talk about with Gretchen telling stories about what her kids were doing and Sara telling things about hers when they were younger.  She found Gretchen very easy and fun to talk to.  Just like Charlie had said.

Gretchen had been yammering on about school and how hard it was to try to help her kids do online school.  She suddenly stopped that conversation and looking at Sara said,

"It's been just me for so long that I'm having fun talking to you.  Hanging around talking to those two, she motioned toward the back porch, just isn't as much fun.  They'd rather talk about sports."

Sara admitted she was having fun too.  They finished making the salad then took it and a plate of fruit and vegetables for everyone to much on while waiting for the rest of the meal.   Just as they sat the things in the middle of the table, Ed brought the plate of ribs over and they sat down to eat.

They talked about how the year was going with the COVID flu going around and how everything had gotten so crazy.  They talked about Sara's accident and how hard her year had started.  Charlie noticed her struggling with using her utensils.  She couldn't use her right hand easily and since she was right handed, she struggled using the left as well.  She often dropped her food off the fork before she could get it to her mouth.  He wanted to jump in and help her but he didn't want to embarrass her either so he left it.

After dinner, they took their drinks and went out on the patio.  The sun was going down and it was a little cooler out there.  Sara brought the dessert out to the patio to have it there.  It was the cherry cake his mom had always made.  One of his favorites.

Sara sat down on the love seat, so Charlie sat next to giving her a warm smile.  He wrapped his arm around her shoulders pulling her close and whispering in her ear,

"See it wasn't so bad.  It told you Gretchen would love you"

She leaned in close to his face, "No it wasn't.  I like Gretchen."  They sat the rest of the evening with his arm around her while they talked with Gretchen and Ed.  Charlie was glad that she and Gretchen had gotten along so well.  Things were going to work out just fine.

# Chapter 20

They had settled into a comfortable routine. Sara had run out of physical therapy visits so had started exercising on her own. She was walking a lot, not long distances on her ankle but enough to get some exercise and strengthen it.  She also had started practicing scales on the piano and doing cross stitch. She had planned to start practicing the piano this year.  She had played when she was younger but had not played for a while.  She figured she could relearn it doing scales.  Since she had the accident, that goal had been put on hold.  However, she found that running the scales for a few minutes every day was helping her hand gain strength and elasticity so she could move it better.  She had also gone back to cross stitch as soon as she could hold the needle between her middle finger and her thumb.  That was also helping.  She noticed as she worked she would curl her hand more to make the stitches and that was also helping her hand to gain mobility.

It was Wednesday night.  Charlie had picked up Sara and they were doing sandwiches at the park. They got out in the open quite often without going places with large crowds.  That was supposed to keep you from getting sick.  They also always wore masks and almost everything they did was just the two of them.

They had eaten their sandwiches and then had walked over to sit on the bench to watch the ducks. Charlie sat laid back with his arm laying comfortably behind her on the bench. Sara leaned against his chest. He liked this position. He could smell her perfume and shampoo and it felt nice to have her lean against him.

"So, Sexy Sara, are you ever going to let me read any of your romance novels?" he goaded.

He knew she was writing them. He had found her website with links to the books. However, he was not going to read them until she was ready to let him. He knew this was a personal thing for her and he wanted to get her permission first.

Sara stuttered, "uh, I guess," she blushed.

"What after all we have done in the bedroom, you're embarrassed for me to read your books?"

"It's not like I don't want you to read them, I just feel too vulnerable." She wouldn't look at him, just wrapped her arms around his chest.

"Sara, I'm not going to do anything.  I love you," he said into her hair.

"I know but it just feels like I'm opening up my heart wide open.  It just is scary."

"We could read them together.  Who knows what might happen"

With that, Sara moved so she could look into his eyes.  He just looked deep into her frightened eyes.

"I guess we could do that" she said softly.

"Why don't you come over tonight and we will start reading?"  he grinned.

Sara's heart was racing, and she felt panicked. She was flattered that Charlie wanted to read her books but it also scared the crap out of her.  It just made her feel like it would open up her heart even more to just be broken.  What if he didn't like them, what if he could see where she had used their love making scenarios in the book?  However, when she looked into his eyes, she had only seen desire and warmth.   He wanted her to trust him.  Maybe it was time to just get it over with.  Pull the band-aid off, so to speak.

She looked into his eyes and murmured, "okay."

They left the park, went to her son's condo to get her things, and then went back to Charlie's. She had saved the books to her tablet so she brought that with her. As she sat next to Charlie on the couch, she started to read.

"Samantha looked at her sexy neighbor standing on the porch with a plate of brownies. He was dark and handsome with a little salt mixed in the brown hair and the prettiest green eyes she had ever seen. She forgot to speak."

Sara continued reading. Charlie listened. When she got to the sex parts, her voice grew quieter but she pushed through. You could feel the electricity in the room. She had felt the tingling in her body when writing the sex scenes, but it was so much more intense with Charlie sitting next to her. He drew her in closer pressing his hand against her hip. He cleared his throat. Before she knew it, he had taken the tablet and set it on the coffee table. Looking back at her, his eyes were dark and so sexy looking. He covered her mouth with his and that was the beginning of the end.

Charlie had kissed her until she could hardly breathe, then he stood up, pulling her with him and headed back to the bedroom where they had the best sex yet.  Maybe having Charlie know her innermost thoughts was a good thing.

Charlie had really wanted to read her books but had not thought about them reading them together until they sat at the park and she seemed nervous when he asked her permission. The idea just popped into his head and it had been a good one.  Even then, he had not anticipated the electricity between them as he listened to her describe the first sex scene.  He wasn't surprised, she had always been willing and gave as good as she got when they were making love but as she described what the characters in the book were doing to each other, all he could picture was the two of them doing those things to each other.  By the time she finished reading the first sex scene, he was hard and so turned on he couldn't stand it.  He took her by the hand and led her into the bedroom where they had the best sex so far.  He now had a better idea of what she wanted and he gave her everything she needed.

Now he lay next to her, both of them breathless and spent.

"Charlie, that was wonderful.  Mind numbing."

"It was wasn't it?"

"I guess having you know my fantasies isn't a bad thing."

He rolled over to look at her.

"See, that's what I was trying to tell you.  I can't make them come true if I don't know what they are."

She rolled over pushing him back down on the bed and putting her head on his chest as she wrapped her arms around him.  He wrapped his arm around her and kissed her on the head.

"Okay, but I think we should read them together."

"Me too," he said as she suppressed a giggle.

# Chapter 21

Charlie and Sara were spending more and more time together.  She was spending a lot of time at his house because they could be alone there and not bother Robby.  She had even gotten so she took her laptop so she could work from his place.  She sat in the family room, he worked from his office but it was nice being so close.  They often took time off to have lunch together.  Sometimes they ate in and sometimes they went out.  The early lunches before physical therapy had been good for their relationship and it was nice to continue those.  Sara also wrote a lot more in the daytime.  Being at Charlies seemed to give her inspiration.  Sometimes at the end of the day, she would read to him what she wrote.  That sometimes ended up with them making love, often before dinner.  Sara was feeling more at home there and Charlie treated her like it was her home.

One day when they had stopped for lunch, Sara brought up the topic of meeting her children.  Charlie was thrilled that she had finally asked him.

"I wondered when you would get around to that but I didn't want to push."

"I didn't want to do it in the beginning because I thought we should see where this was going. However, I'm spending so much time at your place, that maybe it's time."

"I would be glad to meet your kids," he grinned. "Shall we have a barbecue here?"

"That would be fun." How does Saturday sound."

"Great.  You invite the kids and I'll order the food."

"We are ordering food?"

"Just the sides.  I figured you didn't want to do all that with your hand.  I'll make the ribs and it should be fun."

Sara made phone calls to all the girls who were very excited to finally get to meet him.  When she called Robby, he gave her a hard time,

"Nice to hear from you mom.  Here we live together, but I never see you anymore."

"I know, it's not because I don't love you.  I just don't want to cramp your style and here at Charlie's we can be alone."

"I get it mom.  I'm glad you found someone who makes you happy."

Sara told him about the party and he said he would be glad to come.

Last she called her friend Rosie.  They had raised their children together and she thought it would be a good reunion for everyone and then Rosie and Alex could meet the new love of her life.  Rosie had been so excited and insisted on bringing dessert.

Saturday donned bright and sunny.  It was late October which in Arizona meant the weather was perfect.  Sunny days, cool temperatures, and perfect days to have a barbecue.  Charlie had ordered salads and trays of all kinds for the party from the local grocery store.  He picked everything up on Friday night and prepared the ribs so they would be ready to cook the next day.  There was so much food that there was barely enough room in the fridge.

Everyone started showing up at four, all wearing masks because that is what life had become with the COVID pandemic.  Lily and Ryan showed up first with their three. Then Robby showed up and then Rosie and Alex bringing Rosie's chocolate cheesecake.  It was Sara's favorite dessert and Rosie loved to make it for her.  Ivy and Zack were the last.

They were always last.  Ivy had trouble getting things organized to get everyone here on time.  At this point, Sara didn't care.  At least they were all here.

The party was a great success.  The kids had a chance to play with their cousins whom they hadn't seen in a while.  They all talked and laughed and released a little tension that had built up from the virus going around and everyone being quarantined.

Charlie manned the barbecue but still got time to talk and laugh with the kids.  He was also great with the grandkids.  They played kickball in the backyard after dinner and had a great time.  All three children decided they liked him.  Best of all was that they could see how happy he had made their mother.  Each one of her girls hugged her and told her they were glad she was able to go on with life.  Dad was gone, he wasn't coming back and they wanted her to be happy.

Rosie and Alex stayed long after the kids had gone.  It was kind of nice sitting with them on the patio after sunset, talking and laughing.  Just like old times.  Sara was glad that Charlie got along well with Alex and Rosie.  They were her oldest friends and it was important that they all get along.

Charlie had such a great time with Sara's family. He had talked to all of her children and played with the grand kids.  He couldn't really take over as a father, her kids were all grown but he could be a grandfather to the grandkids and he kind of liked that thought.  Was that where they were headed? Evidently, he was.  He was falling in love with Sara and he was looking ahead to them growing old together.

After the kids left, Sara's friends Alex and Rosie stayed to talk.  Charlie had brought out the wine and they ate the cheesecake that Rosie made. It was Sara's favorite and Rosie always made it for her when they had a party.  He had enjoyed the stories about the things that had happened when they were raising the kids.  He had laughed with them and really felt part of the group.  Funny how he just seemed to fit in.  He had expected it to be a little awkward since they had been friends of Roberts too but they accepted him right away.  He really enjoyed their time there and he could see Sara let go and just enjoy herself.  It had been a fun evening and he was glad they had planned the party.

# Chapter 22

It was Wednesday morning and Sara was sitting at Robby's working fervently trying to finish her latest book. This would be her third and she really wanted to get it done. Her phone rang. It was Gretchen. They had exchanged phone numbers when she had dinner at Gretchen's house. They had been exchanging text since then but this was the first time that Gretchen had actually called.

Sara answered the phone wondering what she would be calling for. It didn't take long for Gretchen to explain that she and her mother wanted Sara to go to lunch with them. Just the ladies, she said. Sara knew she would eventually have to meet Charlies mom but she was not sure she was ready. She hoped that she would get along with his mom. Roberts mom had never liked her and never had hidden it. Even at his funeral, she had blamed Sara for his heart attack. She really didn't want that kind of relationship with Charlies mom. Well, all she could do was go to lunch and hope for the best.

When Charlie called that night, she told him about being invited to lunch with his mom. He was glad she would finally be able to meet his mom.

"You will be just fine.  I'm pretty sure she will like you and she is thrilled that I'm finally seeing someone."

"I hope so.  Not sure I can handle another mother-in-law like Roberts mom."

"I think you will get along fine.  I will be working all day; do you want to take my car?"

"Really?"

"Don't look so surprised. I don't have a problem with you taking my car.  You do have a driver's license, Right?"

"Yes, but I'm not sure about driving with my hand.  Maybe if we do that, I should practice."

"Ok, if that would make you feel better."

"I'll also give you my credit card to take with you. Tell them I will pay the bill."

"Will they do that?"

"Yeah, if they know I'm paying."

Sara mused.  "You are such a great guy."

"I know," he laughed.

On Thursday, the day of lunch Sara got up and got a shower.  She had stayed at Charlies last night.  She decided to wear her green knit dress because it looked good on her and she always got compliments about it.  She thought it was important for her to look her best for Charlies mom.

Sara had driven the car a few times with Charlie there to make sure they were safe and she now felt confident enough to drive his truck.  She had agreed to meet them at the café around the corner from Charlie's mom's.  Sara was so nervous as she drove to the restaurant.  What if Charlie's mom didn't like her.  What if she thought he was taking on too much since she was handicapped and couldn't take care of herself?  She parked Charlie's truck in the nearest handicapped spot and hung the window hanger up on the mirror showing her disability card.  She walked into the restaurant feeling a little shy and disoriented at first.  The hostess asked her name then led her out to the patio where she saw Gretchen sitting at a table next to a much older woman.  Gretchen noticed her and stood up as she neared the table.

Sara pulled the chair out from the table with her left hand and sat down, placing her right hand on the table for support and apologizing for putting her arm on the table.

"It still hurts a little if I leave it hanging down and it doesn't have much support," she explained.

Charlie's mom waived it off.

"That's ok, I completely understand.  You've had quite a tough year from what I hear."

Gretchen introduced them but they didn't shake hands because with people just didn't do that anymore with COVID around.  You stayed your distance, didn't hang out with a lot of people and there was no hugging or touching much anymore.

"It is good to meet you, Mrs. Chambers," Sara said.

"Oh, just call me Jean, Mrs. Chambers is too formal."

Just then he waiter showed up to get Sara's drink order, the others already had theirs.  Sara ordered an iced tea with lemon and the waiter hurried off to get it. They talked a little more about Sara's car accident and Charlie's shoulder injury and how their injuries had brought them together.

"I'm so glad he met you," Charlie's mom said.  "I was beginning to worry that he was going to spend his life alone, just because he couldn't get over

Wendy.  She was a nice girl and maybe they would have been very happy, but he didn't really get to live life with her so his memory was of how perfect she was and not reality.  You are the first person that has changed that for him.  That makes you very special."

"Thank you," Sara stammered.  "However, I think he's been good for me too.  He has been so helpful in giving me rides to therapy and getting out and doing things.  We have had a great time and I owe him a great deal for that.  I needed someone like him after all I have been through this year.  The year started off horribly but hasn't turned out so bad now."

"I can tell he really loves you by the way he talks about you and just the fact he seems to be trying to build a life with you.  Shows me that you are different."

"Thank you.  He really makes me feel special even though I feel like more of a burden with all my injuries and stuff."

She patted Sara's arm.  "It's ok.  He has plenty of money and hasn't had anyone to spend it on."

Then his mom went on to share stories about him growing up. Sara loved hearing about how he was as a little boy.  She had laughed and talked with both

Gretchen and her mom like there were old friends. Like family, she thought. Charlie was right again. His mom wasn't that scary and she wasn't judging anything.  She just wanted to meet her.

They ordered lunch then shared a desert between the three of them.  When the check came, Sara pulled out Charlie's credit card to pay.  His mom spoke up,

"You don't have to pay, I'll get it."

"It's Charlies card," Sara said.  "He told me he would cover lunch."

"Well, if it's Charlies card, we will let him pay," his mother said taking the card and putting it in the folder with the bill.

Sara smiled all the way home.  Her life was looking better.  The year may not have started out great but it was turning out fine at the end.

When she got back to Charlie's, she told him about her lunch and how she had really felt like his mom liked her.  Charlie had just taken her in his arms.

"See, I told you it would be fine.  My family is not very judgmental and you are so loveable, how could they not see how great you are?"

Sara smiled then snuggled in close feeling at home in Charlies arms.

# Chapter 23

When Sara woke up on Thursday the bed next to her was empty. It was unusual since they usually went to sleep together, they also woke up together. She got out of bed heading towards the bathroom before she went out to the kitchen to find Charlie. He was sitting at the table looking at the computer.

"You're up early this morning, what's up?"

He finished typing information into the computer before looking up and wrapping his arm around her waist. He pulled her against his chest and said,

"I was thinking we'd take another little trip out of town again."

"Where to this time?"

"How about going to the white mountains? I was thinking we could go stay at the Hon-Dah Resort and Casino up there."

"That sounds like fun, when do we leave?"

"Tomorrow afternoon," he said with a question in his tone.

"That's fine, I can be ready."

She wrapped her arms around his neck and kissed him.  You are such a fun boyfriend.  I like these little trips out of town."

"Me too," He smiled.

Sara worked like a dog all day Thursday and Friday morning so she could get everything done and not have to work on the weekend.  She was all packed and ready to go by three when Charlie wanted to leave.  She did enjoy these little trips and was glad he was thoughtful enough to plan them and take her along.

It was amazing how they had settled into being a couple and doing things together.  It was like Charlie just expected that she would be there and she didn't mind at all.  She enjoyed doing things with him even if it was just having lunch in the kitchen or curling up on the couch for a movie.

The drive to the white mountains was beautiful. This time they headed the other direction down the Beeline highway towards Payson.  The scenery this direction was much nicer than going through Globe. As they drove, the desert landscape changed to lush green trees and forests.  The air got cooler as they reached higher elevations.  It was also mid-December so the weather was a lot colder in the mountains.  Sara shivered a little with Charlie's window open and was glad she had remembered to bring a sweatshirt and jacket with her.  She didn't always need them in Phoenix, even in December. Sara reached back in the seat to get her jacket. Charlie offered to close the window, but she told him it was fine, she would just put the jacket on.

The Hon-Dah resort and casino was on an Indian Reservation but was supposed to be nice and have beautiful views.  Sara was excited to see it.  Since it was on the Reservation, they would also be able to gamble a little.

The drive was only a couple of hours so they were able to check into the hotel and then go to dinner after arriving.  After dinner Charlie wanted to do a little gambling.   They headed into the casino. Luckily there weren't a lot of people there.  They had less people sitting at each of the tables and empty chairs sectioned off between those sitting there.  You also had to wear a mask the entire time you were in there.

Charlie was interested in black jack but Sara was not sure she was good enough to play.  He handed her a twenty and told her to play some slots if she wanted.  She took the twenty but stood by him for a while watching him play.  He was doing well and making a little money.  Finally, her ankle started bothering her from standing on it, so she wandered off to find a slot machine and a chair.

A couple hours later, Sara had a bucket full of money and decided to cash it in.  Turned out she made sixty dollars on top of the twenty Charlie gave her.  She found him still sitting at the table with a pile of chips in front of him.  His eyes lit up when she saw him.  He finished the game and then cashed in his winnings as well.

"How did you do?" he asked.

"Not too bad.  I made forty bucks."

Sara started to take the money out of her pocket to give him back his twenty.

"No, you keep it," he smiled.

Charlie had won a couple hundred dollars.

"This will almost pay for our trip," he said.

He stuck his money in his pocket and wrapped his arm around Sara's waist as he led her back to their room.

*****

Charlie had a good time playing black jack but he'd had enough time alone without Sara.  The purpose of this little jaunt was to spend some fun time together out of the city.

He opened the door to the room and let Sara walk in first before closing the door behind them.  As he closed the door, she turned toward him with that sexy little smile on her face.  The one that made it so he couldn't refuse her.  She reached up, wrapped her arms around his neck, and kissed him deeply.  He wrapped his arms around her waist, pulling her against his hard on.  God, she turned him inside out.

He felt her smile against his lips as she felt him hard against her belly.

"A little turned on, are we?" she teased.

"Honey, you have no idea," he growled as he drug her across the room to the bed with her giggling all the way.

 He loved when she giggled like that.  It made him feel good to know she was happy.

She lay on the bed with her clothes still on.  She still looked so sexy.  He laid down next to her and took her breast in his mouth and sucked on it through the fabric of her shirt.  Her breast got hard and he gently tugged on it with his teeth.  She groaned and squirmed underneath him.  He smiled and took the other nipple in his mouth.  Another groan.  He could see her hips move out of the corner of his eye.  She was turned on and having trouble holding still.  He liked her that way.  He reached down and undid the button on her jeans and pulled them off along with her panties.  He stood and took his own pants off standing in front of her wearing only his shirt.

He reached down between her legs.  She was nice and wet.  He knew that older women often had trouble with that, but so far Sara didn't.  He covered her body with his pushing slowly little by little until he filled her completely.

"Charlie, that feels so good," she cooed.

He kissed her delving into the sweet corners of her mouth.  She tasted so good.  He started moving his hips.  As he slid in and out, Sara's breathing grew labored.  Her hips moved in rhythm with his.  He started kissing across her cheek and then nibbled on her ear.  Licking the sensitive spot down her neck.  She moaned.

God, that moan almost threw him over the edge. He managed to hang on until Sara reached her

climax.  She arched her back and called out his name.
He couldn't hold on after that and with one more
push, filled her before collapsing on top of her.

It took him a minute to catch his breath and he rolled
over to the side pulling her over with him and holding her
against his chest.  He loved holding her in his arms.  She
wrapped her arms around his chest and they lay there for
quite a while before moving under the covers and curling
up to go to sleep.

*****

Sara woke up fairly early the next morning.  The
sun hadn't come up yet.  She watched Charlie
sleeping next to her for a minute or two.  He was
such a handsome sexy man.  She was lucky to have
met him.  She slipped out from under the covers and
headed to the bathroom.  Charlie was still asleep
when she came out so she got dressed in jeans and a
t-shirt then pulled a sweatshirt on before going out to
the balcony.  It was a bit chilly outside but she loved
watching the sun come up and the scenery in the
mountains was beautiful.  Evergreen trees as far as
she could see.  She watched a little squirrel run up the
tree closest to the balcony.  It was so relaxing to be in
the mountains and watch the wildlife.

She heard the door open behind her and Charlie's arms wrapped around her from behind.  He pulled her back against his chest.  She felt safe and warm in his arms.  He nestled his face in her neck and whispered.

"Good morning, Sexy Sara."

She felt a shiver down her body and it wasn't from the cold.  He didn't move, just held her.

After a while, he whispered, "Are you hungry?"

She smiled and turned around, cupping his face between her hands, and kissing him.

 "Yes, I am starving."

They headed down to the restaurant for breakfast. It took a while to get into the restaurant.  The restaurant had to space people apart so could not fill all of the tables.  They had an empty table between each table that had someone sitting at it.  You were also required to wear masks into and out of the restaurant and only take them off to eat.  All of the waiters were wearing masks and gloves.

After breakfast, they wandered through the gift shop looking at all the Native American art.  Sara loved that about living in Arizona.  All the great art.

The rest of the day was spent driving through the mountains, enjoying the scenery and each other's company.  They stopped at a little café for lunch.  As usual it was wonderful food and they had a great time.

The evening was spent curled up together, watching a movie and ordering room service.  Sara thought it had turned into a perfect weekend.

Sara and Charlie left the next morning as soon as they got up.  They were back by eleven just in time to see a women leave Robby's still wearing a sexy little black dress that she obviously wore the night before.

Robbie had walked her to her car and turned around just to see his mom and Charlie drive up.  His face was bright red at seeing his mother.

Sara just smiled and said, "You are 30 years old. I'm just glad I'm not cramping your style."

# Chapter 24

The holidays were drawing near.  This was a real challenge this year since it was not a good idea for everyone to get together.  A lot of people decided they were going to do it anyway but Sara was not sure that was such a good idea.  She decided that she and Charlie would get together but suggested that they make all the dishes they wanted to eat and then plan to have dinner at a certain time. Anyone who wanted to join in could connect through a zoom meeting.

The girls decided that might be ok.  They would hopefully be able to have dinner with both Sara and Charlie as well as their husbands families that way. Sara invited Robby to come over if he wanted since he was alone and they could still social distance with just the three of them.

Sara bought a small turkey which Charlie helped her to cook.  He had to lift the pan in and out of the oven since her hand couldn't hold that much weight. He also helped her with the sides and the pies.  They had decided to eat at one so Charlie logged into zoom at ten minutes to and the others joined one by one. Charlie also invited Gretchen, Ed, and the kids to join in and they did.

It was really different but it was kind of fun. Everyone took a turn talking about what they were thankful for by taking a turn standing in front of the computer.  It was fun to see the grandkids and then they were able to talk and laugh together while they ate.  Sara hoped that they only had to do this one year because she did miss hugging the kids but this was better than having people end up sick or dead.

Many people had not been so careful.  They had big family parties. Many people traveled across the country in airplanes and the airports were packed. The downside of all of this was that the COVID numbers increased dramatically after the holiday and suddenly all of the hospitals were full of sick people. Many ICU's had no room for injury patients.  Many cities had to close down again in order to bring the numbers of sick people down so that hospitals could take care of them.

# Chapter 25

Sara decided for Christmas it was still to soon for them to have a big family party.  She decided to do what her grandmother had done and make up boxes for each of the families and then she and Charlie would deliver them on Christmas Eve.  There were a couple of toys for each of the kids.  She normally would have made them but she hadn't been able to do any of that this year, so she had purchased them online and had them delivered. She had a package of a dozen tamales for each family.  That was kind of an Arizona tradition and she had ordered them the day after Thanksgiving.  She also had homemade sugar cookies.  She had been unable to decorate them this year because of her hand injury so they were just frosted in white and red and green.  She had added some oranges and a package of nuts and then a present for each of the adults.  They had her two daughters and Gretchen's family, then she made a special box for Robby since he was not married and had no children yet.

They waited until dark so that there was less chance of being caught then headed out to drop the packages on the doorstep then leave.  She had gotten this idea from her grandmother who had done this when she was a child.  The big difference was that her grandmother had done it in the snow and she and Charlie were in Arizona where there was no snow.

Charlie had gone along with the idea.  He thought it was a great idea, especially since everyone was quarantined.  Sara had included Gretchen and her family and Charlie was so excited.  Sara had packed all the boxes and put names on them.  She sat in the car while Charlie put the box on the steps then rang the doorbell and ran.  As he came running back after the first box, he jumped in the car and they headed off.  He was huffing and puffing.

"This ringing the doorbell and running was much easier when I was younger," he laughed.

"We could put the box on the doorstep then call them after you get back to the car."

"Hell, no!  There's no fun in that."

So, they continued on delivering the other boxes. When they got to Robbie's, he was last and they waited for him to answer the door.  Sara had been a little concerned about him spending the holiday alone, but he had told her he had plans with someone. When they got to his condo, he had a girl there with him.  He introduced her to his mom and Charlie and then they left him alone.

"I guess I shouldn't worry so much about my son, he has everything figured out."

"Yes, we just need to get you out of his house so he doesn't live with his mom."

Sara laughed.  "It's not like I spend much time there anymore.  I'm at your house most of the time."

"So, maybe we should make it official and move all your stuff over to my place."

"Hmmm, Maybe."

# Chapter 26

Charlie had enjoyed delivering Christmas presents to the kids.  He had fun ringing the doorbell and running.  It was a lot more difficult at his age but he still felt the excitement of hurrying not go get caught just like he had as a kid.

They got back to his place about nine.  It was still fairly early and since it was Christmas eve and they didn't really have much to do the next day, they made hot chocolate with peppermint schnapps and chocolate liquor with whip cream and a peppermint stick.

Charlie turned all the lights off except the Christmas tree and they curled up together on the couch to talk and enjoy the evening.  They talked about their favorite parts of Christmas.  Sara told Charlie about her Christmas's as a child.  She explained that her grandmother had done boxes like they had done tonight every year.  She said she always looked forward to the box showing up.  It usually was not marked that it came from her grandmother but you could tell by the smell of the things inside.  He grandmother had a fireplace and everything smelled like grandma's house.  She told him about the year she peaked and got the gray coat with the white fur collar.  She had wanted it really bad and was so excited she had to check under the stairs where her mom had hidden everything.  Her mom had been so mad because it had been her best Christmas ever.

Charlie told her about his Christmas's as a boy.  The year he got his bike and the next year a sled.  Gretchen had been so much younger than him, that for many years, he had been an only child.  After Gretchen came, he had to pretend he believed in Santa Clause even though he had outgrown it by then.  However, his dad had made it fun and let him help buy and put out the gifts for Gretchen from Santa.

Charlie had really enjoyed spending the evening talking about their childhoods.  It was things they had never talked about before but it made him understand her a little better.  By the time they finished their stories, it was after ten.  Charlie got up and pulled a present from under the tree.

"This," he said, "is for you to open tonight."

"I don't need to open a present tonight.  Shouldn't we wait until tomorrow?"

He grinned mischievously and shook his head.

"No, we both need this one tonight."

Sara took the package as Charlie sat back down next to her and opened it to find a white negligee with red bows.  It was just in her size.

A smile spread across her face.

"Oh, I see what you want."

"Go try it on.  I want to see it.  I've been waiting weeks for this night."

Sara laughed then got up and took the negligee with her to the bedroom to change.  When she came back out and stood in the doorway, she felt a little silly, but Charlie was looking at her with excitement and interest.

"You look gorgeous," he said gruffly.  Then he stood and walked towards her with a great big grin on his face.  He wrapped both arms around her and kissed her.

"I knew you would look beautiful in that."

He then took her by the hand and led her back to the bedroom where he laid her back on the bed so he could see her.  He gazed at her lovingly and she reached her arms up towards him.

"Come here big boy, she whispered.

He took off his clothes all except his shorts and laid next to her on the bed.  He began tracing the lace straps on her shoulder following it down to the lace that went across her breast to the little red bow in the middle.  He continued on across the other breast and up the other strap.  Just that sensuous touch made Sara's body heat up.

"God, I love you," he muttered under his breath then her took her breast in his mouth and sucked it through the lacy material.  She arched her chest towards him and pressed his head tighter against her chest as she rubbed her fingers over his head.  He switched to the other breast and she wiggled her hips twisting over towards him.  He pressed her hips back against the bed with the palm of his hand.

"No, baby we are doing this slow tonight."

He traced his finger from the red bow between her breasts down between them and to her belly button. She squirmed with the feel the lace between his finger and her body and it increased his excitement even more to see her response.  He traced his finger over the lace on her hip where the high cut panty lay on her hip.  She was now stretching to meet his touch.

She whispered, "Charlie, I need you."

"I know baby."

He continued to trace the lace across her hip and down between her legs, rubbing the sensitive skin on her upper thigh and staying away from her sensitive folds.   She moaned.

"God, I love when you make that sound."

He changed sides and ran his finger over the lace on the other hip and down inside her thigh.  She moaned again and he could feel himself getting hard with her response to his touch.

He slid his finger under the fabric between her legs and touched the soft wet folds.

"Oh, Baby," was all he could say.

He slid a finger inside her just as she grabbed hold of him with her hand.  He had not expected that and it sent a shiver of pleasure throughout his whole body.  It almost did him in but he maintained control enough to unsnap the fabric between her legs and moved over her.  He filled her completely with one push.

"Charlie," she yelled his name.

Another push and she arched toward him as she reached her orgasm and he spilled inside her. He collapsed on top of her.

After a few minutes he rolled over pulling her against him.  She wrapped her arms around him and mumbled, "This has been the best Christmas ever,"

"Yes it has and I'm glad I spent it with you."

# Chapter 27

They had made it through the holidays and spent New Year's at a party thrown by Rosie and Alex. Sara enjoyed getting together with Rosie and Alex. They had lived next door to each other for thirty plus years until her husband had died.  She really missed having Rosie around all of the time.   They had decided it would be alright to get together since it would just be the four of them.

Rosie was a great cook and they had finger foods of all kinds that Rosie had put together.  Mini quiche, cocktail shrimp, spinach and artichoke dip with crackers, nuts, a veggie tray with ranch dip, ham rolled with pineapple cream cheese, celery with cheese, deviled eggs and peach iced tea.  The food was fantastic.  They talked and laughed and played games.  Charlie had also enjoyed it.  He fit right in as if he had always been part of the group.  In fact, Sara thought he fit in better than Robert. Sara had been a little worried about that, but they didn't seem to mind him at all and they all had a great time.

Just before midnight, Charlie got out the champagne they had brought and Rosie got out the glasses.

The four of them gathered in the living room to count down the last 10 seconds to the new year. Charlie was sitting next to Sara on the love seat with the champagne in one hand and his other arm wrapped around her waist. They cheered when the new year 2021 was here.  Charlie clinked his glass against Sara's then leaned in for the celebratory kiss.

"This year may have started out bad, but it turned out fantastic because I spent it with you."

Alex stood next to Rosie with his arm around her and made a toast to a much better year in 2021.

Sara knew it would be better because she now had Charlie.

*****

As he drove home after the party with Rosie and Alex, Charlie looked over at Sara.  She had laid her head back against the seat and closed her eyes.

"Are you falling asleep on me again?" he joked.

"No, I'm just resting.  I'm too old to stay up this late," she laughed.

"I hear you."

He reached over and took hold of her hand. Threading his fingers in hers, he gave it a little squeeze.

"I know your year didn't start out great, but I think the year turned out fantastic.  Never in a million years would I have thought I would meet someone like you.  You made the end of the year awesome."

She looked over at him and smiled.

"I have to agree.  You were the bright spot in a very bad year. I love you Charlie."

"I love you too baby."

# Chapter 28

The next morning Charlie woke up before Sara. He looked over at her next to him in his bed. She was sleeping peacefully and she looked beautiful. She is exactly where she should be, he thought. He leaned over her and kissed her at first gently, but then as he deepened the kiss, she opened her eyes and then he felt her smile against his lips.

"Good morning beautiful," he mumbled.

"Good morning handsome. What a way to wake up in the new year."

"I thought you would like that. We have some unfinished business to welcome in the new year. You were too sleepy last night."

She smiled, "Sounds like fun."

After they made love, Sara was laying with her head on Charlies chest and their arms were wrapped around each other.

"I've been thinking a lot about us. I think you should move in here with me. I know it's just a formality, me asking you since you spend most of your time here anyway, but I think we should make it official."

"Are you ready for me to do that?" She looked at him inquisitively.

"Yes, I am." Charlie smiled and rubbed her cheek before kissing her.

"I love you. I like having you around and I can't imagine things any differently."

"I would love to," she smiled and kissed him.

The next Saturday Charlie helped her pack up the rest of her things in boxes so they could be easily moved.  She had already moved a lot of her clothes and things she used daily over to Charlies.  There were some storage items and some kitchen things she had to move over but they were already boxed up. Ed, Charlies brother in law, and Ryan, and Zack, Sara's son in laws all came over about noon to help Robby get the little bit of furniture and boxes put in the truck. Charlie ordered Pizza and they all sat and ate before loading the truck and heading out.

After they left the girls helped vacuum and clean the bathroom.  It wasn't that she had to clean like she would if she were moving out of an apartment but she didn't want to leave a mess for Robby to have to clean up

After the men had emptied the truck, Charlie came back to get her and Sara hugged all the kids and told them they were welcome at Charlie's anytime.

Charlie corrected her.

"It's your place now.  They are always welcome at their mother's home."

Sara smiled at him with tears in her eyes.  He made her feel special.

They climbed in Charlie's car and headed home.

On the ride home, Charlie reached over and put his hand on her knee.  It was amazing how it still sent shivers through her even a year later.  He smiled at her.

"I'm so excited you agree to move in with me.  I never dreamed in a million years that I would be in this position but I'm glad I met you.  I couldn't imagine life any without you."

Sara smiled back, putting her hand on his.

"Me either."

When they got home, Sara noticed a tan SUV in the driveway.

"Who is that parked in our driveway?"

Charlie grinned at her. "That's a surprise."

"A surprise?" she didn't understand.

"Yes, that's yours."

"Oh, Charlie," was all she could say.

He finished. "You need a car. This way you don't have to wait to use my car or for me to drive you there. You can go wherever you need to go. I figured you needed a little freedom."

Sara looked at him with tears in her eyes. "Charlie you are so wonderful. What did I ever do to deserve you?"

"You deserve to be happy my dear. I'm just glad I can help with that."

"Can we go for a drive in it?"

"We certainly can."

He took the keys out of his pocket and gave them to her.

She jumped out of the car and climbed into her new car. She started it then waited for Charlie to climb into the passenger side.

"Where shall we go?"

"How about to dinner?  I'm starving."

She drove to Charlie's favorite steakhouse where they went on their first date.  It only seemed fitting since it was another first for them.  The first meal after Sara moved in.

That night, they made love in their new home.

# Chapter 29

It was May almost a year since Charlie had given Sara a ride to physical therapy.  He had planned another little trip for them.  He had enjoyed all the trips they had taken together but this one was going to be special.  Charlie had planned it all himself.  Making reservations at a B&B in Sedona.  He had let Sara know he had a surprise for her and she needed to take a few days off.

He was so excited; he could hardly stand it but he managed to maintain control because it was going to be a very important trip for them.

They left after lunch and Charlie headed up I-17 towards Flagstaff.  As they headed out of the city, he looked at the Arizona desert.  It was actually quite beautiful once you got used to the cacti and the sand.  Since it was May there were still wild flowers blooming everywhere and some of the cacti were also in bloom.  Lots of bright color everywhere.  He reached the turn off to highway 89 A which was a scenic detour through the mountains before getting to Flagstaff and the way to Sedona.

Sedona was unique in the way that it had a lot of deep red color in the sand and mountains surrounding it.  Because it was higher elevation it was also much cooler.  There were plenty of trees in the canyons.  Box Elder, Willow and Oak trees.  Pinyon pines and Juniper.  It was all very beautiful.

Sara had made several comments about how much she liked driving through Sedona.  She talked about sliding down slide rock here as a kid.  Slide rock was a natural water slide made by the run off of a glacier in Oak creek Canyon.  It was a very fun slide even though the water was very cold because of the glacier.  It was also rough on the clothes since you were sliding on rock.  It wore out jeans really fast.

Charlie remembered going there as well.  He might try to take her there while they were here.  He didn't imagine at their age they would be sliding down it, but it would be fun to see.

Charlie drove through town and then to the B& B on the other side.  They checked in and found the room to be nice and cozy with a balcony hanging out over oak creek.  It was a beautiful setting.  As they stood on the balcony, he noticed it was a little chilly.  Good thing he had told Sara to pack warmer clothes.  It was already getting hot in Phoenix but they might need jackets and sweats up here.  They stood for a while watching the water run along the creek bed.

There were birds fluttering about and squirrels running up and down the trees.  It was very beautiful and relaxing.

At five, they started getting ready for dinner. Charlie had made reservations at the Canyon Breeze restaurant.  It was supposed to have a great view.  He had told Sara to dress up.  When he walked out of the bathroom to see her standing in the room wearing a silky black dress, he couldn't help himself.

He sucked in a breath, "You are gorgeous," he exclaimed.

Sara blushed, "Thanks."

He took her in his arms.  "You are the sexiest woman I know."

She looked deep into his eyes, "You aren't so bad yourself, sexy man."

He pulled away, "We better go."

He didn't want to let go of her.  What he really wanted to do was to make love to her but that would have to wait.  They had important plans.

He helped her into her coat and they walked to the car with her arm wrapped through his.

When they got to the restaurant, they were led to a table near the window where they could see the creek and the beautiful trees.  He had asked for a beautiful view and kind of secluded where they could be alone.  The restaurant had been able to do that.

Charlie was as nervous as a school boy asking a girl on their first date.  He knew he had nothing to worry about but for some reason he was still nervous.  Maybe because he wanted it to be perfect.  He ordered a bottle of wine and they decided what to order from the menu.

Sara ordered a chicken salad and Charlie an enchilada.  While they waited for their food they talked about the last year.  How they had met, what they were both thinking about when Charlie had offered a ride and how they were both glad that he did give her a ride.

"I was so distraught," Sara said.  "I was feeling all alone and here comes this handsome stranger to help me by giving me a ride.  Who knew that it would lead us to this."  She smiled, tears welling up in her eyes as she spoke.

Charlie reached across the table and took her hand.  He looked into her eyes.

"I'm glad I decided to give you a ride. I had seen you in physical therapy and thought you were beautiful and sexy but I was not sure how to get to know you. Luckily, I didn't have to figure it out. I had an opportunity that presented itself. Like it was meant to be."

"Well, I'm just glad you did. I have had a wonderful time with you. I love these little trips we take. They have really been so much fun."

The waiter showed up with their meals and they ate. They talked more about the trips they had taken and the things they had visited.

Sara brought up all the little trinkets he had bought her to remember their trips by.

Charlie said, "I have loved just being with you. Spending time with you has been the best. Especially making love to you. I hope that I can do that forever."

Sara smiled and looked into his eyes. "I hope so too."

Charlie then reached in his pocket and pulled out a package. He held it up.

"I'm not going to get down on one knee because I'm just too old for that,

"Sara Miller, Will you marry me?"

Tears welled up in Sara's eyes again and she whispered,

"Yes, Charlie Chambers, I would love to be your wife."

Charlie took the ring out of the box and put it on her finger.  It was beautiful, a simple single diamond and looked like that was where it belonged.  Sara started up at Charlie with tears in her eyes.

"Sorry," she whispered.  "these are happy tears.  I never thought I would be this happy again."

Charlie just held her hand and let her cry.

They finished their dinner and then went back to their room.

Charlie closed the door behind them but couldn't wait any longer.  He took her in his arms and kissed her.  Covering her mouth with his he claimed her, delving into her mouth with his tongue he poked into every corner of her mouth.  She tasted wonderful and he would never ever get enough of her.  He reached back and unzipped her dress, letting it fall to the floor.  She was wearing a red lace bra and matching panties.

"sexy was all he said.

He ran his thumb across the tip of her breast making her moan with his touch.  God, he loved when she made that noise.  It made him hard and sent fire surging through his body.  Sara unbuttoned his shirt then pressed her hands against his chest, rubbing her hands across his chest over the nipples that got hard with her touch.  It was his turn to moan.  He reached around and undid her bra pulling it off her arms and letting it drop to the floor.  He reached down, taking her nipple in his mouth he sucked it hard getting a second moan from her.

"Oh, Charlie," she moaned.  "That feels wonderful"

He backed her over to the bed, laying her back on the quilt.  He looked at her as he undid his pants and dropped his pants and shorts to the floor and ripping his shirt off.  He couldn't take his eyes of her; she was so sexy laying there.

He again took her nipple in his mouth and sucked and licked it until she was moaning his name over and over.  She started to squirm and he reached down into her panties and pressed his finger against her clit. He massaged it in circles as she gasped and her hips started to buck.  She looked into his eyes with complete love and trust.  He loved making her feel good and it made him feel good as well.  He continued to massage her clit and slipped a finger inside her as she continued to buck.  She started to say something but nothing came out as she opened her mouth to speak.  He slipped another finger inside, curling his fingers against her g spot and she raked her head back against the bed and cried out his name.

Charlie moved up next to her, wrapping his arms around her and holding her until she started to relax. She wrapped her arms around his chest and whispered.

"I love you Charlie."

"I love you too baby."

He kissed her on the head and pressed her body against his.

She leaned up on one elbow to look in his eyes. She reached in and kissed his lips.  Pressing her tongue inside his mouth.  He could no longer stand it.

He rolled her back over on her back and moved between her legs.  Pressing against her center, he pressed just enough for her to feel it but not enough to really go inside.  She moaned.

"Charlie, I need you."

"Baby, I need you too."  He pressed hard all at once pushing in all the way.  She gasped and then smiled.

"Oh, that feels good."

He started moving his hips in and out until she gasped in short little gasps and moans.  She arched her back and pressed her head back against the bed again as she climaxed for the second time.  She was beautiful when she came.  He pressed in again deeper this time and reached his own climax, spilling his seed into her before collapsing on top of her.

He lay there for a few minutes before he could regain enough strength to roll over next to her.  When he did, he pulled her over on top of him, wrapping his arms around her and pressing her head against his chest.

She was finally his and they could spend the rest of their lives doing this.  He had never been so happy.

# Epilogue

The wedding was in May twenty, twenty two.   They
had decided to wait a while to get married so that the
worst of COVID was over and they could enjoy
getting together with family and friends and not have
everyone end up sick.  There had been so many
stories of family gatherings and weddings where
many of the guest ended up sick and dying with
COVID.  They didn't want that on their conscience.
It had been almost two years since Sara and Charlie
had met.  It had been a wonderful two years and even
though they had been living together and enjoying
life, they also wanted to be married.  It was a small
wedding, just family and a few close friends.  They
decided to have it at the Hon Da resort because it was
in the white mountains and a little cooler than
Phoenix.  They had been able to get a package deal
so that everyone could stay at the hotel.  They didn't
have a wedding party as such.  Just pretty pink and
mauve dresses for Sara's daughters and
granddaughters.  They included Gretchen and Evie in
that.  The girls all helped Sara get dressed.  She
decided not to buy a new wedding dress, she just got
a pretty light pink dress that made her look beautiful.
Ed stood in as the best man and held the rings.

The day turned out perfect.  Perfect weather, sunshine but not the scorching heat of Phoenix.  Sara walked down the aisle on the arm of her son.  As she walked down the aisle, she looked straight ahead gazing into Charlie's eyes.  He had a nice smile.  He was beautiful and sexy and she was glad to have met him.  The reception was fantastic everyone dancing and having a great time.  Sara and Charlie had danced a little but Sara still had some trouble with her ankle and so she mostly sat and watched her children and grandchildren dance with each other and have a good time.

After the toasts were done and everyone was back dancing and enjoying the party, they snuck back to their room to be alone.  After all that was what a wedding was all about, for them to spend the rest of their lives together.

The next morning, they got up early and headed out to Napa Valley for a winery train ride and tour of several wineries.  They had a two hour drive to the airport in Phoenix where they caught a plane to Sonoma County then picked up a rental car to take them to the train.

Sara was so excited.  She had never been on a train like this before.  She was excited to see the napa countryside and taste the wine.  Most of all she was excited to have another trip with Charlie.  These trips had become their thing and she really enjoyed spending time with him.

They finally made it to the train.  The train was made up of real old time restored pullman cars.  It was luxurious with dark paneling, brass accents, and plush arm chairs.  They are their meals as the train traveled through the countryside.  They heard stories about the wine train, tasted wines from all over the region and saw some beautiful scenery as they traveled from winery to winery.

They visited love lock bridge that originated in China.  They bought their own lock and hung it on Love lock bridge.  The tradition was that it would lock your souls together.

It was a wonderful trip.  Sara had enjoyed every minute.

*****

Charlie had gone along with the Napa Valley wine train because Sara had wanted to do it, but he had to admit he had enjoyed it as well.  The best time was holding her in his arms at night.  It was the perfect beginning to a new life together.

www.ingramcontent.com/pod-product-compliance
Lightning Source LLC
Chambersburg PA
CBHW071419150726
48000CB00001B/406